Ambi-dangerous

Longarm shook his head to say, "Won't be no next time. You don't get up from this table, leaving your suckers to pay the piper."

Ashton shrugged and answered, simply, "You won't try to stop me if you know what's good for you. Agreed?"

Longarm said, "Not hardly. I said you were under arrest and I meant what I said. Do you aim to come quietly or feet first?"

Ashton snarled, "That's it! You may fire when ready, Rosemary!"

So Rosemary fired, then fired again, because she knew a .32 whore pistol fired with limited stopping power and her target was a very large man. As Ashton went down and writhed on the floor at their feet, the sexton moved closer to finish him off with a heavier dose of lead.

Rosemary, aiming the loaded revolver in her left hand at Longarm, quietly asked, "Did I mention I happen to be ambidextrous?"

TABOR EVANS

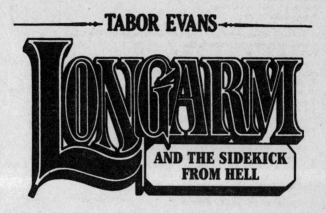

LONGARM

AND THE SIDEKICK FROM HELL

JOVE BOOKS, NEW YORK

THE BERKLEY PUBLISHING GROUP
Published by the Penguin Group
Penguin Group (USA) Inc.
375 Hudson Street, New York, New York 10014, USA
Penguin Group (Canada), 10 Alcorn Avenue, Toronto, Ontario M4V 3B2, Canada
(a division of Pearson Penguin Canada Inc.)
Penguin Books Ltd., 80 Strand, London WC2R 0RL, England
Penguin Group Ireland, 25 St. Stephen's Green, Dublin 2, Ireland (a division of Penguin Books Ltd.)
Penguin Group (Australia), 250 Camberwell Road, Camberwell, Victoria 3124, Australia
(a division of Pearson Australia Group Pty. Ltd.)
Penguin Books India Pvt. Ltd., 11 Community Centre, Panchsheel Park, New Delhi—110 017, India
Penguin Group (NZ), Cnr. Airborne and Rosedale Roads, Albany, Auckland 1310, New Zealand
(a division of Pearson New Zealand Ltd.)
Penguin Books (South Africa) (Pty.) Ltd., 24 Sturdee Avenue, Rosebank, Johannesburg 2196,
South Africa

Penguin Books Ltd., Registered Offices: 80 Strand, London WC2R 0RL, England

This is a work of fiction. Names, characters, places, and incidents either are the product of the author's imagination or are used fictitiously, and any resemblance to actual persons, living or dead, business establishments, events, or locales is entirely coincidental.

LONGARM AND THE SIDEKICK FROM HELL

A Jove Book / published by arrangement with the author

PRINTING HISTORY
Jove edition / June 2005

Copyright © 2005 by The Berkley Publishing Group

ISBN: 0-515-13956-4

JOVE®
Jove Books are published by The Berkley Publishing Group,
a division of Penguin Group (USA) Inc.,
375 Hudson Street, New York, New York 10014.
JOVE is a registered trademark of Penguin Group (USA) Inc.
The "J" design is a trademark belonging to Penguin Group (USA) Inc.

PRINTED IN THE UNITED STATES OF AMERICA

10   9   8   7   6   5   4   3   2   1

Chapter 1

It felt like a great getting-up morning as Deputy U.S. Marshal Custis Long of the Denver District Court strode for the federal building along sunny sandstone walks. There was a cloudless sky of cobalt blue with a west wind off the nearby Front Range holding the summer heat at bay. Stenographer gals on their way to work ahead of him giggled and jiggled in their summerweight skirts under spring bonnets of straw, bedecked with artificial flowers, and all seemed right with the world as Longarm mounted the granite steps to the imposing south entrance.

Which only served to show you cannot judge a day by its cover.

For as he topped the stone steps he found his way blocked by a beefy blond cuss who looked like he was trying out for a part in one of those gloomy grand operas by Mr. Wagner, save for the ten gallons worth of Stetson he had on instead of a winged helmet and the low-slung, tied-down Dance Brother's six-gun he carried instead of a sword.

Walking around a strange kid blocking your way into the schoolhouse can get things off to a poor start. It seemed a tad early to walk on through before the blond cuss had his say, if he had anything to say. So the two of them just stood there a long tense time before the big blond cuss said, "I understand they call you Longarm and you think you're pretty good."

To which Longarm, as he was, in fact, better known in those parts, could only reply with a modest smile, "You can call me anything but late for breakfast, and what's my opinion next to that of others I've had this same dumb conversation with, stranger?"

The Viking dressed more like a Texas rider said, "I would be the one and original Buchanan T. Skane. The *T* stands for Trouble. I allow my friends to call me Buck."

"Do I call you Buck or Trouble?" asked Longarm in a curious tone.

Skane said, "I'm still working on that. If you're so good how come I see you're packing your own gun cross-draw under that sissy suit you got on? Didn't your momma never tell you a side-draw beats a cross-draw ever' time?"

Longarm calmly replied, "Let's leave our mommas out of this. I don't aim to say that again. We can blame this store-bought suit on President Rutherford B. Hayes and the federal dress code drawn up at the suggestion of his first lady, Miss Lemonade Lucy, who got rid of all the White House cuspidors and won't abide strong drink nor Anglo-Saxon verbs in her vicinity. The cross-draw rig was my own decision after I found out how a side-draw drew in some positions. So I'll tell you what. You allow me to carry my gun my way and I'll not say a word if you decide to dangle that Dance from your dong."

The operatic Texan slapped leather.

Then he stood very still with his hamlike fist on the ivory grips of his holstered gun for a long breathless moment.

Miss Bubbles from the stenographic pool asked in a shocked tone, "Custis Long! Why are you pointing that silly gun at that poor man?"

Longarm kept the muzzle of his .44-40 trained on

Skane's chest at point-blank range as he mildly replied, "I was just fixing to ask him about that, Miss Bubbles. Why don't you go on inside whilst me and old Buck, here, work things out?"

The aptly nicknamed Miss Bubbles sniffed, "Men!" and headed inside with a flounce of her Rainy Susie skirts. Buchanan T. Skane licked his lips and asked in the boyish manner of a bully whose bluff has been called if his old pal Longarm couldn't take a little joshing.

Longarm said, "Let go them fancy gun grips and let me put this point forty-four to forty away before somebody calls for the law. You are still alive because I assumed you were too smart to go for broke with a federal lawman on the steps of this federal building. On the other hand, John Wilkes Booth shot Lincoln serious in front of a whole lot of folk who knew him."

Skane let go his grips, muttering, "Aw, shoot, I was only trying to show you how good I was."

Longarm holstered his own weapon as he dryly remarked, "So now we've established that, I hope, for all time. If you ever go to draw on me in the future I may not hold my fire. Idiots waving loaded guns in my face get me tense. Is there anything else we have to talk about out here? My boss, Marshal Vail, gives me hell for reporting in late without a mighty good reason."

The bluff blonde, who seemed to want to be called Buck after all, confided, "That's what I started out to talk over with you, Longarm. Your boss is my *padrino*. When I told him I'd come up here to Colorado to be his senior deputy, he allowed he already had one. Namely you. I figured if you was willing to stand aside and let me be *El Segundo* for a few months I'd be on my way to Easy Street."

Longarm replied, "It ain't up to me, Buck. Let's go on up and ask the one who cuts and deals such cards."

As he led the way inside, the big Texican puppy-dogged along, explaining how he'd served as a range detective

3

down home but been turned down by the newly reorganized Texas Rangers, adding in a hurt tone, "My own daddy rode with Uncle Billy Vail under Captain Big Foot, back when all anybody asked was how good you might be with a gun. Nowadays they got all these fool tests they expect you to take. Seems you're supposed to know the written laws of Texas before they allow you to be a Texas Ranger. Ain't that a bitch?"

Longarm replied, not unkindly, "Since President Hayes took over, us federal deputies are required to savvy and support the Constitution of these United States. Didn't your godfather mention this to you, Buck?"

Skane said, "I fear I walked out in a huff when he said I'd have to start at the bottom as a junior deputy if I started at all. That happened last night at his place up on Capitol Hill. By the cold gray dawn it came to me that if I could get you to sort of volunteer out of my way for just a few months I'd be able to move on up the way that earlier Denver district deputy did, to chief of police and all."

As they mounted the marble steps together, Longarm smiled thinly and observed, "If we're talking about Denver's current Chief David J. Cook, be advised it took him more than a few months as a federal deputy to apply for the job. After serving in the Colorado Cavalry and the military police, old Dave served as a Denver city marshal for three years and a federal deputy for ten."

At the head of the stairs, Longarm added, "If you mean to take old Dave's job away from him, be advised he stands six foot three and lacks this child's sense of humor. The office is down this way."

Most of the crowd was headed the other way toward the courtroom and law offices down at the other end. As they bucked the current, the beefy blond Skane continued, "I never expected to gain higher office up here in damnyankee country. My point was how old Dave Cook made out so grand after gaining more modest fame as a senior deputy.

4

I'll bet they'd let *you* be the chief of police in some place like Cheyenne or Salt Lake City if you applied for the position, right?"

"The thought has never crossed my mind," replied Longarm, truthfully.

Skane said, "Us poor working stiffs take all the risks for less than half the pay. I've had more than one cow thief peg a shot my way in the field and a range detective rides for little more than a buckaroo."

"It's a cruel world," Longarm conceded as he opened the oak door with gilt letters reading U.S. MARSHAL WILLIAM VAIL.

Inside, they found old Henry, the kid who played the typewriter and kept the files, pounding away in triplicate on a sandwich of onion skin and carbon paper.

Buchanan Skane grinned loftily down at the seated clerk to snort, "I give up, what is it?"

Henry stared back with the expression boys reserve for worms as they scrunch them onto fish hooks while Longarm explained, "What we have here is nobody you want to fuck with if you mean to ride for this outfit. Old Henry makes up the bonus vouchers we rate for warrants served, prisoners transported and so on."

Henry said, "Aw, you've gone and spoiled all my fun. Marshal Vail's waiting on you both in the back. He wants to talk with you alone, first, Custis. So why don't you leave the one and original Buchanan T. Skane of Val Verde County out front with me as I quiver in my boots?"

Longarm laughed, pointed at the bench reserved for waiting and headed on back as Skane asked Henry, "Who told you I rode for Val Verde County a spell back, ah . . . Henry?"

To which Henry lightly replied, "Val Verde County. I'm paid to check job applications. Yours failed to mention your getting fired for sleeping on duty as a jail guard."

Longarm didn't hear the rest of it. He was lighting a

three-for-a-nickel cheroot in self-defense as he made his way back to the oak-paneled, smoke-filled inner sanctum of the somewhat older and way shorter and stockier Billy Vail.

He found his boss, as expected, seated amid billowing fumes of expensive but dreadful cigar smoke behind a good-sized desk that simply wasn't big enough for all the wanted fliers and telegraph messages piled atop it in a jumble only Billy Vail, himself, dared to paw through.

There was one horsehair-stuffed leather chair on Longarm's side of the desk. Longarm sat down uninvited and, seeing there was still nothing like an ashtray on his right or left, flicked tobacco ash on the threadbare rug without comment.

Billy Vail said, "Your pneumatic stenographer, the one they call Miss Bubbles, beat you here by minutes to tell me about the scene in the doorway downstairs. I see you had him down as a moon calf with delusions of ferocity, too?"

Longarm shrugged and replied, "He claims you're his godfather. That ain't why I held my fire. He told me you were his *padrino* as I was putting my own gun away. I know this is none of my beeswax, boss, but how could you have let such a silly thing happen, if such a silly thing happened?"

Vail smiled sheepishly and said, "Me and my mind were younger, his dad was a pal of mine and his ma seemed normal, too. All I ever did was stand by the font whilst they sprinkled their retarded child. How was I to know he was fixing to turn up as the answer to an even bigger pain in the ass after all these years?"

Vail exhaled an octopus cloud of dreadful smoke and added, as if he really meant it, "I'm swearing him in as a probationary junior deputy. The two of you will be working together, undercover, over on the west slope of the Front Range. New mining camp called Pot Luck."

Longarm quietly but firmly replied, "No, we won't. I've established I work best alone because even with a backup man who knows his ass from his elbow, it means I've got two backs instead of one to cover. Buchanan T. not only told me but convinced me that *T* stands for Trouble. He's a bag of wind fixing to get his fool self blown away at any moment. He's a compulsive bully packing a Confederate antique in a tied-down buscadero rig with neither the brains to avoid a needless showdown nor the *draw* it takes to *win* one. Henry just intimated he was a low-paid turnkey fired from a county jail for sleeping on the job. So why in thunder would we swear him in for undercover work in the field?"

Vail replied, expansively, "We wouldn't. Or, least ways, nobody would *expect* us to. So that's why we're *fixing* to. They'll be worried about a cuss like *you* and you're getting to be well-known along the Owlhoot Trail. But as tall, dark and handsome as you may be, one tall tanned cuss can pass for another, with a change of duds, a few days without shaving and a more noticable cuss strutting out front and doing most of the talking for the two of you. Who's likely to expect the quiet member of the team might have brains to pour piss out of his boots if they see he's taking orders from an obvious asshole?"

Longarm said, "I don't like it. I'd rather take my chances in a wig and fake whiskers. He's a loose cannon. There's no saying what he might do or say because I doubt he knows his ownself."

Vail said, "We're agreed on his total lack of qualifications. Seeing you know what I think of him, too, you'll be able to read between some lines as I fill you both in on your mission. Get him in here so's I can explain the same and give you both your field orders at the same time."

Longarm rose, sighing, "Damn it, boss . . ." But life was too short to waste time arguing with a woman or a boss. So Longarm went back out front to fetch Buchanan T., or as it was easier to describe him, Buck.

On their way back to Billy Vail's office, Longarm snagged a bentwood chair from a conference room and sat it closer to the door as he waved the big beefy blonde to a seat on padded leather.

Billy Vail waited until they'd both settled down before he nodded at Skane and said, "Like I told you up to the house last night, *ahijado mio*, we do not as a rule put the sons of old pals in charge of shit before they've shown us what they can do, starting at the bottom of the totem pole. But rules are made to be broken when an unusual situation comes up. So try this on for size . . ."

He leaned back to pontificate. "The mushrooming mining camp of Pot Luck on the Leadville narrow-guage line is named for its first strike, which assayed as an icing of gold quartz atop a thicker layer cake of lead and silver carbonate."

"Like Leadville," Longarm said, nodding.

It had been a statement rather than a question so Vail went on. "As is ever the case, slickers with clean hands and dirty minds have moved in to prey like leeches on the men who moil for gold. Nobody paid much mind to the usual hard-luck tales of swindles, extortions and claim-jumping until a crusading newspaper man and more than one prospector complaining on paper about claim-jumping turned up missing."

Skane asked with a puzzled frown, "So what? Since when has it been a federal offense to jump a mining claim?"

Billy Vail looked pained but patiently explained, "Since the General Mining Act of 1872 replaced an earlier confusion of state and federal rules and regulations. You file a homestead claim with the Bureau of Land Management and a mining claim with the Bureau of Mines, both of 'em under the direction of the Secretary of the Interior, along with Indian Affairs, Geological Survey and such."

Waving his evil black cigar the way a teacher might wave a pointer, Vail went on, "Local law and order are left to state, territorial or local courts and such lawmen as might be on hand. Since mining claims are filed with and kept by the federal government, guess why Washington asked for Custis, here, by name."

Longarm said, "I give up. Why me and not some geology professor?"

Vail said, "It's your own fault for cracking them other cases in the bowels of the earth after everybody else seemed stumped. Some regular investigators were already sent up to Pot Luck. They had no luck. Far as they were able to determine, those charges were baseless and all those missing men may come home someday, wagging their tails behind them. So now they want me to send you in and, seeing you solved all those other cases in mining country, somebody might be *expecting* me to."

Pointing the cigar at the big blond Texican, Vail said, "Anybody who knows shit about this office knows how few Wagnerian Vikings we have on our current payroll. I want you to act as the nominal head of the team, Buck, doing most of the talking, signing most of the papers and such. Do you have any trouble with the notion that Deputy Long, here, will actually be calling the shots?"

His big goofy godson grinned and allowed, "Not as long as everybody *thinks* I'm the boss!"

Billy Vail took a drag on his smoke, not daring to meet Longarm's eye.

Longarm managed not to grin like a shit-eating dog.

It wasn't easy.

Chapter 2

Mining men from Leadville Johnny Brown to Silver Dollar Tabor and no doubt a mastermind or two spent as much time in Denver as up by their holdings in the nearby Rockies. So lest they be remarked on as an odd couple leaving Denver together, Billy Vail sent Buck Skane out with old Henry to establish his own cover while Longarm tried to sell the Larimer Street Bridge to Reporter Crawford of the *Denver Post*.

As he was fixing to leave, a few minutes after Skane and Henry had left the federal building, Longarm told Billy Vail that, once he'd tracked down his newspaper pal, he meant to interview a local mine owner he knew about current gossip up along the Front Range.

Before Billy Vail could ask him who he had in mind, Longarm switched them to another track by opining, "It ain't going to work. The man's an asshole with a big mouth and a chip on his shoulder!"

Vail chortled, "I noticed. I want 'em all watching *him*, not you, as the two of you get established in Pot Luck. I don't want you to ask one question about irregular transfers of mining property as you wiggle your way into the local scene. After you boys make a strike and file a claim, somebody ought to be approaching you, if there's anything to all this sinister bullshit. How were you figuring on making such a lucky strike, old son?"

Longarm shrugged and said, "No sense working up a sweat. What if we were to buy a bottomed-out claim nobody else wants, offering, say, a gallon of rye and renaming our new mine the Gallon of Rye?"

Vail nodded approvingly and asked, "How do you aim to salt her? With a shotgun blast of gold dust?"

Longarm shook his head and said, "Too crude. If there is this mastermind amassing mineral rights, he's a mining man, not a pilgrim on a quest for El Dorado. I figure it might make the bait more tempting if the local assay office told us poor simps we had a marginal lode running less than a hundred dollars a ton, with a ton or so blasted and mucked in case anybody wants to look."

Vail nodded and said, "Just the sort of ore a bigger outfit with its more modern methods would find tempting. You're fixing to disolve some bullion in *aqua regia* and sprinkle it on the shattered quartz?"

Longarm rose to his considerable height, saying, "Won't work along the Front Range. This mine owner I'll be talking to later put me on to some new slickery that ain't as well-known. But right now I have to scout up Reporter Crawford so I'll get back to you before I leave town."

It worked. Vail never asked and so Longarm never had to fib. It was a tad early for the free lunch at the nearby Parthenon Saloon, but Longarm knew Reporter Crawford liked to turn up early, lest he miss anything as the locals assembled from the surrounding business or government office buildings.

But when he got there, Longarm found the place night empty. So he ordered a beer from the well-endowed barmaid and killed some time asking her if she knew she looked just like Virginia Woodhull, the famous suffragette who advocated Free Love.

Meanwhile, down on Curtis Street, Henry was explaining why nobody on a secret mission to a mining camp wanted to show up in a ten-gallon hat.

Holding up the peaked wool cap he'd rummaged from the bargain table, Henry explained, "Nobody wears a broad-brimmed hat down a mine and you have to admit these peaked caps are more dashing than derbies."

Skane protested, "I'd look like a sea captain or some Russian Jew in a hat like that, for Gawd's sake!"

Henry said, "Greek fishermen wear them, too. They're popular in our Rocky Mountain mines because the bill keeps drip water out of your eyes and shades them from the head lamp you'll be wearing if you wind up way down deep."

Holding on to the cap he'd chosen for the bigger man, Henry waved it toward the back and added, "We have to fix you up with mining boots, now. Steel-tip toes and sensible heels, dubbed waterproof with wool-wax. You can't wear those spurs on this mission, either. New blue denim stands out. We'd better fix you up with dark whipcord and drag them through the dust outside before you put them on."

They were arguing about that as portly Reporter Crawford entered the Parthenon Saloon in his checked suit under a jaunty derby. Longarm nodded politely but didn't wave him over, so naturally Crawford came, following his nose for news.

Longarm let the newshound draw him out, a grudging admission at a time, until he suddenly looked concerned and said, "I swear I've already had too much and it ain't High Noon yet. Forget what I said about that field mission to Montana, pard. It's supposed to be . . . confidential."

Reporter Crawford assured Longarm his readers would never read a word from him about Denver's answer to Wild Bill headed up to Montana with a warrant on a sex offender. He agreed there was no delicate way to report the offense

12

of a reservation school teacher who sucked noble savages, even as he was rewording things fit for publication.

As if chagrined at his own loose lips, Longarm changed the subject to Miss Virginia Woodhull and her scandalous notions. Reporter Crawford said he'd heard the sass and her free-loving sister had been seen riding bicycles in those shocking outfits invented by Miss Amelia Bloomer, speaking of crazy ladies.

And so time was killed until the place was too crowded for easy conversation and Longarm left, fortified by pickled pigs feet and devilish eggs. For if the Parthenon Saloon charged a tad dear for drinks, they sure spread a grand free lunch.

Henry was putting Buchanan T. Skane aboard a local to Lyons, with stagecoach instructions to the gold camp called Jimtown, as Longarm made his way to a sign shop near the federal building. The big blond Texan said he didn't see why he wanted to go north of old Jimtown only to head southwest towards the same.

Henry patiently explained, "If you aim to work with Longarm be advised he's sneaky. Nobody backtracking you to Jimtown is likely to hear you arrived from the direction of Denver if you never did, see? You're to check into Mother Mahoney's boarding house near the stage station and stay out of trouble, or try to, until your sidekick, Canada Cooper, gets there in his own new mining duds."

"Longarm hails from Canada?" marveled the big blond Texican.

Henry started to explain how many riders of the Owlhoot Trail might have been advised to watch out for a tall, dark cuss from West-by-God Virginia. But he decided the less Skane had to spill the less likely he'd be to spill it.

Longarm was playing his own cards close to his vest as he entered the sign shop to howdy the little gray gnome he already knew from over in the federal building. The old-timer was forever scraping off and then reworking the gilt lettering on all those oaken doors. One time when Longarm had been pulling court duty they'd had a long conversation whilst the sign painter immortalized a new federal prosecutor in gold.

Getting right to the point, Longarm explained, "I'm in the market for a hundred dollars worth of that gold leaf you letter with. You told me that time there was barely an ounce to one of those . . . books, did you call them?"

The old-timer nodded and said, "You're talking about a dozen books at the current rate. Gold is only worth twenty dollars an ounce as raw bullion. The price of gold leaf is mostly in the making. Takes a gold beater with considerable skill a lot of time to hammer gold thin enough to see the sun through."

Longarm smiled incredulously and said, "Go on, we're talking about solid heavy metal."

The old sign painter reached under his counter, saying, "See for yourself," as he produced what resembled a black leather-bound bible at first glance. He opened it to gingerly lift a single sheet of waxed paper out, saying, "Don't breath on this. Don't touch the gold leaf. Just take it outside and hold it up to the afternoon sun."

So Longarm did, holding the thicker sheet of paper with its thin burden of gold leaf like a flaming candle as he moved over to the door to follow the old man's directions.

Out on the walk, he carefully moved the wax paper above his head to shade his eyes against the glaring afternoon sun. He muttered, "I'll be damned!" as he stared up at a dim but clearly visible purple sun for a spell. Then he went back inside to allow, "This gold leaf is sure beat thin. How come the sun looks purple through yellow gold?"

The sign painter explained, "Gold stops and bounces back the yellow light, allowing its opposite, purple, to sneak through. That's how you can tell real twenty-karat leaf from cheaper substitutes. If the sunlight's not purple, or you can't see it at all, you're holding up an alloy. So how come you need that much gold leaf, Deputy Long? You're not going into the sign-lettering business, I hope?"

Longarm said, "Not hardly. Could you bill, say, a dozen books to my office and not tell anybody else I was ever in here? I don't want anybody to know I've got such bodacious stuff on me as I head out in the field on a secret mission."

The old-timer laughed and lined the books of gold leaf up on his counter as he decided, "You're going to salt a mine, right?"

Longarm knew better than to bluster. He sighed and asked, "You heard?"

The older man who dealt with tiny traces of gold every day shrugged and admitted, "This is the first I've heard of using gold *leaf*. They usually load gold dust or shavings into a shotgun shell and fire into a pile of ore. Let me guess. You're going to wrap gold leaf around sticks of dynamite, shove them in boreholes and set them off inside the solid rock and . . . I don't know, son. You'd wind up with microscopic flakes of gold imbedded in particles of shattered rock. Would your average sucker ever notice?"

Longarm proceeded to put the gold leaf away in his side pockets as he replied, "I hope not. I'm banking on an assay man who talks too much picking up on the color when he runs his acid test. I hope you understand we never had this conversation?"

"What conversation?" asked the older man with a wink.

It was still early when he stepped back out in the sunlight. Longarm considered taking his purchases home to his furnished digs on the less fashionable side of Cherry Creek. But the less he was seen around his usual haunts for a spell the less anybody was to remember seeing him, and he'd never met a gal who didn't like to look at gold.

So it was barely midafternoon when Longarm presented himself at the front door of an imposing brownstone mansion on Sherman Street with a nosegay of store-bought forget-me-nots,

The maid-of-all-work who was only there during the daytime made him wait in the hall whilst she saw if Madame was receiving that afternoon. Madame was, in her front parlor, armored in a buttoned-up bodice and Dolly Varden skirts of purple velvet. After that she stood five foot two on the comfortable side of thirty with her light brown hair piled high atop her fine-boned head as she smiled uncertainly with iced-tea eyes that made him thirsty.

When she asked to what she might owe the honors at that hour, Longarm asked if she knew the sun was shining on her outfit through a sheet of gold leaf.

That worked. The young widow of an old mining man who'd died with a smile on their honeymoon told her maid to put the violets in water and led Longarm to a seat as she asked with a Mona Lisa smile what on earth he was talking about.

As they down together by the bay window for the edification of any nosy neighbors, Longarm got out that first book they'd already opened and handed her that same loose sheet, saying, "See if you can hold this up to yon sun without detaching the gold leaf. It's stuck on natural with that static electricity. Hold it so's the gold is uppermost."

The bemused widow woman did as she was told. It only took her a moment to observe, in a delighted tone, "I see what you mean, Custis! Why does the sun shine so purple through this gold?"

Longarm explained as she handed the leaf back. She asked how they ever got gold so thin you could see the sun through it. Up at her late husband's mines near Leadville the gold came out of crushed quartz less refined.

Opening the book on the cushions between them, Longarm told her what that old gilt letterer had told him. "They put a flat square of gold betwixt two sheets of a sort of parchment they call gold beater's skin. Then they beat it,

16

just so, until the original square has squashed out flat to the edges of the gold beater's first square of skin. Then they cut it into quarters and beat each thinner square into a wider, thinner square and repeat the process over and over, to where the original square of gold has been beaten into more than a hundred thinner squares. They tell me it's time to stop when you can see the sun shining purple through a leaf."

She laughed. "Heavens to Betsy! You mean there are only a few cents worth of gold in the lettering across the window of my bank?"

He said, "That's about the size of it. Each sheet is only a few molly clues thick. I'm hoping a molly clue here and a molly clue there might add up to gold quartz just worth mining at your average assay house. I was wondering if you'd heard-tell of that new gold strike called Pot Luck northeast of Leadville?"

She said, "Of course. Is that what brings you to my door so early, you brute? I thought I was going to have to defend my fair white body!"

Longarm calmly replied, "It's early. Hoping we might have time to jaw about Pot Luck before your maid leaves for the day."

She allowed they did. Longarm knew he wouldn't have to swear her to secrecy. That was one of the advantages of carrying on a socially unacceptable secret affair with a pillar of Denver Society. She wanted it known she barely knew the tall, dark, handsome lawman who'd helped her mine crew catch those high-graders that time. She had to be nice to him, of course, but as to any other cases he might be working on, well . . . really!

So he asked right out if she'd heard-tell of some mastermind out to amass all the proven claims around Pot Luck for some mysterious reason.

She said, "I've only heard the usual complaints. I'm supposed to be out to jump the claim another widow holds

17

on a bottomed-out try hole a mile from one of my holdings. As for why anyone would want to jump all those claims, there's no mystery. You wind up rich when you amass a lot of mineral rights. How soon might that mean old Billy Vail send you out of town on me?"

Longarm said, "Anytime, now. They sent a sidekick I'll be working with ahead of me this morning. I'll be joining him in Jimtown, where the two of us will prospect some for the record before drifting south to Pot Luck with a few days worth of beard, needing a bath. I can't say what happens then. Don't know what we'll find waiting."

She gasped. "You have to leave *tonight*, for heaven's sake?"

He said, "Best if I drift into Jimtown in the wee small hours, off a late night stage, with no crowd hanging 'round."

The buttoned-up widow woman sprang to her feet, saying, "Let me get rid of that fool maid so the two of us can get out of this ridiculous vertical position, then!"

Longarm didn't argue. Life was too short and he'd been hoping she might say something like that.

Chapter 3

As most consenting adults discover the first time they shack up for a spell, of all the positions they're bound to try, the position best for conversation, short of stopping, has to be dog-style.

So as Longarm donged her dog-style, inspired by the wonderous sight of her bare behind in broad daylight, the widow with the light brown hair was saying, "Custis, dear, I've been thinking. You don't have to waste time up in Jimtown if you want to be accepted as a down-on-your-luck mining man, drifting in from mining country. We're expecting labor trouble up around my Leadville holdings. What if I fired you in public as one of those union agitators, after giving you time to grow some stubble at my mountain lodge?"

Longarm turned her on her back to finish right, so they couldn't talk since his tongue was in her mouth for a spell. But once they'd shared a long shuddering orgasm and had come up for air, he naturally asked what sort of trouble she was talking about.

Snuggling her naked charms against him as he lit a smoke for the two of them, she said, "Oh, you know, the usual stuff . . . about three times the wages of a cowboy not being enough for a hard-rock miner. Governor Pitkin says if they strike he'll send in the guard to protect mining property and it ought to blow over in no more than a month."

Longarm got the cheroot going before he muttered, "Damn, I wish we'd known that this morning. I'm already too famous in the Front Range for my own good. Leadville toughs drifting into Pot Luck just as me and my Texican are setting up as mine owners could be just what the doctor never ordered!"

He inhaled a drag, let it out as he passed the cheroot to her and morosely told her, "Fat's in the fire, now. Orders are orders and tempting as your offer sounds, I got to meet up with that other cuss in Jimtown. If there's trouble in Leadville by the time we drift down to Pot Luck, we might want to hold off on opening another mine to picket."

He took the smoke back as he sighed, "I wish they wouldn't do that. But you don't get far as an agitator acting with common sense. The last time the so-called Knights of Labor acted up they flooded one-man try holes with no hired hands on their payroll and burned a boarding house run by a poor old gal who'd never owned a mine in her life."

The widow began to toy with his manhood as she replied, "Goody. Tell Marshal Vail you don't want to go and stay here with me."

He kissed the part of her hair and said, "Don't *want* to go. *Have* to go. Speaking as one mine owner to another, how would you go about amassing all the claims in your district without leaving a paper trail? I mean, sure, you can trick, extort or murder the original owner out of a claim and hold it apart from others under any number of false fronts. But soon as you consolidate all them claims into one big mining operation, won't that leave your mastermind exposed to public view?"

She began to draw him to attention again as she demured, "Only if you're a crudey with no lawyers and brokers to call your own. You've heard of the Comstock Claim Jump, of course?"

He said, "Sure. Hasn't everybody? It was famously raw. Couple of dumb, innocent prospectors named O'Riley and McLaughlin struck it rich on the east slope of the Sierra Nevada back in '59. They were digging away at a lode assaying a thousand dollars a ton in gold and three thousand in silver when this brazen old loafer, Henry Comstock, came into their camp at Caldwell's Spring to inform them they were mining his claim."

"Who went to jail?" the mine-owning widow demanded.

Longarm thought and remembered. "Nobody. There was plenty to go around if they agreed to share and share alike. They soon had two more partners, one being the Old Virginny Virginia City was named after. The other being a Manny Penrod whose exact reasons for a one-fifth share were never quite clear. Then old George Hearst horned in to establish his fabulous fortune by buying out McLaughlin, who continued to prove how stupid he was. Hearst recouped the thirty-five hundred he paid McLaughlin his first day as an owner. Comstock, himself, was suckered out of his stolen shares for not much more. Easy come, easy go. They say Old Virginny was bought out with a bottle of booze and a blind horse. Pete O'Riley was the only one of the original five who held out for real money, if you call forty grand real money. A year later Virginia City had a population of ten thousand and went on to take Bismarck's Prussia off the silver standard and finance the Union through the war."

"And who went to jail?" she repeated.

Longarm said, "I follow your drift. Get all the paper in separate piles in the names of stooges, swap 'em back and forth through holding companies and such with the fine print made up by slick lawyers and CPAs more than once, and who's to say who did what, with what, and to whom way back when?"

She didn't answer. She'd been taught it wasn't polite to talk with mouth full and, what the hell, he knew the answer.

She begged him to stay the night. But he was on his way just after sundown, traveling light and, not needing as many changes as Buchanan T. had, starting out less cow from scratch. His well-broken-in low-heeled army boots would attract less attention than high-heeled Justins and move him about faster than new mining boots might. He already had clean but faded blue denim and an old army-blue work shirt. He'd grabbed his own billed cap of black wool when he'd made his way home to pack. The hardest change he had to make was to a second-hand gun rig: a less battered Schofield Smith & Wesson, chambered for the same substantial .44-40 rounds made by the same firm. The Schofield or Army Model Mark Three fired single-action while reloading faster than any other revolver on the market and it was, hence, the weapon of choice for as many gunslicks as Longarm's more usual but unfortunately famous double-action Colt. Mayhaps a tad more accurate because of its longer barrel, the Schofield broke open like a shotgun with a push rod ejecting all spent cartridges at once so's you could reload in a flash, snap the cylinder and barrel back in place and resume what you were doing, single-action or not. The James-Younger gang was said to swear by the Schofield. Longarm hoped they knew what they were talking about.

He never let the double derringer at one end of his watch chain show. So he figured they could come along. He reloaded other possibles in his saddle roll, with those books of gold foil nestled in the core, slung the same over his shoulder hobo-style and was on his way.

The local train ride up to Lyons had him riding a night stage to the southwest before midnight and he dropped off in Jimtown, out in the middle of nowhere's much, around three o'clock in the morning.

It was just as well he knew where he was. No mining

camp ever shut down all the way, of course, what with three shifts working 'round the clock underground. But Jimtown was little more than a wide spot in a mountain road with weedy second growth aspens whispering in the dark. Somewhere a night bird was sobbing its poor heart out as the stage rumbled on for the camp called Ward.

Mother Mahoney was in bed at that hour with a boarder of her choice. But a fat, sleepy-looking Kimoho breed of the female persuasion let him in and showed him to the room Buchanan T. had already checked into.

Buchanan T. was still awake. So was the skinny old drab he was in bed with. So Longarm trimmed the lamp he'd lit as soon as he hung his roll over the head of his own bed.

The big blond Texican said, "I'm sure glad you're here. I've been waiting on you with some embarrassment. Could you let me have a dollar to pay this lady so's she can be on her way?"

"You owe her a whole dollar?" Longarm marveled as he reached in his jeans for a cartwheel. He'd been funning, but old Buck explained, "We agreed on two bits. But you took so much time getting here . . ."

Longarm waited until the raddled whore had been paid off and sent on her way before he asked, "Didn't Henry send you off with some travel expense money, Buck?

Skane said, "A hundred in cash. He said you'd be coming along with a lot more. I . . . ah, lost it at the saloon across the way. Bucking the tiger."

"You got yourself into a *faro* game this late in the nine-teenth century?" Longarm shouted, adding, "Couldn't you find a wheel of fortune or a pal called Doc with three wal-nut shells and a magic pea?"

As he hung his new but shabby gun rig over a bedpost and sat down to shuck his boots, Longarm asked what name they might have their new mark down as.

The beefy Texican said, "Henry said to use my real name, seeing as I ain't known as a lawman up this way and

23

might forget some made-up name. He told me you'd be going under a total disguise."

Longarm said, "Canada Cooper. At your service."

Skane said, "Oh, yeah, Henry told me. I'd forgot. Can I go to sleep, now? That old gal gave me quite a ride, once I told her I required a dollar's worth of her charms."

"She likely felt flattered," Longarm muttered, not wanting to deflate the kid by opining it had likely been some time since any man had paid her for more than a blow job and if he came down with the clap it would serve him right.

Skane never answered in words. He was already snoring. That was yet another thing to admire him for.

But what the hell, it had been a long day and no man who'd served a hitch in any army was kept awake by snoring. So Longarm caught about five hours sleep before they rang the breakfast bell downstairs, and Mr. Thomas Edison claimed to have invented phonographs and electric lights on four hours' sleep a day.

Mother Mahoney seemed to need more sleep than the boarders she hadn't been sleeping with. Another breed-gal presided over the breakfast of bisquits and gravy, served with cheap but strong coffee. There were six other gents and a lady present. One of the gents asked old Buck in a jovial tone whether he meant to have another go at the tiger across the the way.

Skane glanced sheepishly at his pal, "Canada," to opine he was starting to have doubts about that faro deck.

Longarm wasn't the only one there to smile wearily. They called it bucking the tiger because way back when faro decks had come with tigers prowling their backs. You hardly ever saw such decks in big cities such as Lyons or Leadville, these days. Word had gotten around that a few dealers marked the tigers with extra-skinny stripes betwixt the printed ones they came with. But there was much to be said for the company of such a moon-calf when he stood out in a crowd and might be remembered, from up Jimtown way down in Pot Luck.

Being the quiet member of their team, Longarm only said enough to establish they meant to prospect over by that Trapper's Rock they'd heard so much about.

A mining man who'd been there longer said, "Ain't no color over near Trapper's Rock. It's been prospected a heap, seeing it's a granite outcrop one can see for miles, and vice versa."

Longarm knew that. He'd been up that way before, albeit he was better known in Ward than Jimtown. He wasn't out to strike color. He was out to leave some lasting impressions well north of Pot Luck and men tended to remember those they laughed at.

Later that morning they left Jimtown with a hired burro and packed dinner grub, bound for Trapper's Rock. They took a good stiff hike through mostly second-growth aspen punctuated by small stock spreads. Mining camps were more spread out because you found more just plain rock than rocks worth turning over in the Rocky Mountains. Nobody much lived over towards Trapper's Rock, so-called because back in the days of the beaver trade mountain men had felt more secure holed up in such natural forts.

Knowing what was there, Longarm didn't make them hike all the way to the big bowl-shaped outcrop where rainwater pooled natural. He only had to give old Buck more pocket jingle and instruct him in secrecy on the ways you could wind up broke in a mining camp.

Hunkered off the trail in a shady glade he'd visited earlier with a total stranger to the Front Range, Longarm explained, "When we get back, it's okay if you want to get laid, and I want you to be a sport about buying an occasional round at the bar. But the U.S. Government can't afford the way you gamble. So cut it out."

"Am I supposed to act like your boss in town?" Skane asked hopefully.

Longarm said, "You're supposed to take the lead in springing for the drinks, buying supplies for us and such. Don't try to bully me. Others are as likely to wonder why as they are to admire either of us. In sum, just be your naturally noisy self and most will remember you as my . . . senior partner."

The Texican said, "*Bueno*. What am I directing you to do out here amid all these trees, *segundo mio*?"

Longarm said, "It don't matter. Gold is where you find it and there's no set way to look for the same. We just want to establish we're mining men *looking* for the shit before we drift into Pot Luck, looking for more."

Skane grinned like a mean little kid and asked, "Wouldn't it be a pisser if we was to *find* us some gold, pretending to just look for gold?"

Longarm smiled at the picture and allowed, "Stranger things have happened. You hear tales of prospectors searching for lost mules and striking it rich. They told Ed Schieffelin he'd only find a tombstone to call his own, out in unexplored Apache country, and look what happened."

"What'll we do if we really strike gold up here in these hills, pard?" asked the boisterous Skane.

Longarm said, "Don't count your chickens before they're hatched. If they were easy to find, neither gold nor silver would be worth so much."

"Yeah, but what if?" Skane insisted.

Longarm shrugged and said, "I reckon we'd be allowed to file a claim on it. It's a free country. But don't hold your breath."

And so things went, with the big kid prattling on and on about what he'd do if ever he had his own gold mine, and then they were back in Jimtown just in time for supper.

Supper came in the form of boiled potatoes and mummified mutton with stale donuts for dessert. Billy Vail wanted them to stay in Jimtown for at least seventy-two hours. They figured to be long hours, indeed.

Longarm didn't tag along after old Buck and his new-found friends as they headed across the way to see if whiskey might cut the taste of mutton fat. Even if he hadn't been sick of Skane's dreams of fame and fortune, he wanted to be remembered in Jimtown as little more than a hard-to-recall backup man.

So he was perched on a porch rail out front, smoking, when he found himself in the company of that one gal boarding there. He already knew her name was Hazel and she was up there to teach school as soon as they finished building her one. After that she was blandly pretty with hair that matched her coffee-colored dress. She wore it in a tight bun atop her head. Her eyes were dishwater gray. When he asked if she minded him smoking, she allowed his cheroot smelled nice.

She perched on the other rail across from him and neither of them said anything for a spell. Then Hazel said, "I knew you were shy, like me. Is that why you let that big blond boy lord it over you, ah, Canada?"

Longarm said, "Oh, Buck don' exactly lord it over me. I just don't have as much to say, is all."

She sighed and said, "I know what it feels like to be at a loss for words. I thought I'd walk up to the general store and see if some soda pop might wash down the taste of that supper. Would you care to join me?"

He said he surely would, and as they strolled up the road in the gathering dust, he decided the next few days might prove more interesting than expected. For she sure talked a blue streak for a gal at a loss for words and by the time they got to the general store he was walking arm in arm with the shy little thing.

Chapter 4

The next couple of nights couldn't have worked out better with old Billy Vail pulling puppet strings from his desk in Denver. The first time she fucked him, Hazel sweetly but firmly warned Longarm she expected him to shave more regular if he meant to go on fucking her in the woods. As a schoolmarm in a tiny town, Hazel had to be careful about her rep and said they shouldn't appear to be spooning back in Jimtown. As a schoolmarm who'd been guarding her rep a *spell*, Hazel had half dragged him to a fern-lined nest she'd discovered amid the aspens on her lonely earlier explorations. She wanted to be on top, rocking on the heels of her high-button shoes with her hair let down and her dress flung over a clump of dwarf cedar. The nights were crisp at all seasons at that altitude. But she said they had their love to keep them warm and she just hated it when lovers got all sweaty.

Next morning at breakfast Hazel ate across from him as if butter wouldn't melt in her mouth and referred to him as Mr. Cooper the one time she asked him to pass the syrup.

Longarm and old Buck spent the day prospecting for color out in the woods. Along the way Buck bragged on having backed down the bully of the town in that saloon.

He chortled, "Dumb Irishman famous for knocking others out with his fists. You should have seen how he crawfished when I whupped out my old pissoliver, explained it was a Dance Brother's revolver and made him dance a spell before I ordered him to just git and stay got whilst we were in town."

As they strode along through dappled shade, Longarm said, "I wish you wouldn't tell gents *we* were at feud with them before you informed this child, Buck. What were you and the other asshole fussing about?"

Skane said, "Oh, you know, growing boys just naturally want to know where they stand with one another. He intimated I didn't know shit about prospecting and when I suggested all the gold he'd ever seen had been in his momma's mouth when she offered to suck him off, he invited me to go outside with him. He bitched it wasn't fair to pull a gun on a man who'd invited you to Fist City. But he danced just the same when I nicked the toe of his boot with my first shot."

Longarm sighed and asked how the dance lesson had gone over with the rest of the saloon crowd.

Skane said, "Oh, some just stared, poker-faced, whilst others laughed a heap. It usually goes like that."

Longarm said, "I know," as he ran a thoughtful thumbnail along the stubble of his jaw. He asked for more details. But Skane didn't know how many brothers the bully of the town might have, where he worked, where he lived or whether he had a rep for gunplay in the past.

When Skane confessed he hadn't worried about such shit, Longarm told him, "You'd best start. It just ain't smart to start up with strangers you don't know, Buck. They tell a tale of a Texican named Joe Grant. Blew into Fort Sumner early in '79 and proceeded to throw his weight around. The details vary with the telling. Joe Grant doesn't seem to have been a man who worried about details. He bragged a heap on his wonderous ways with a six-gun to what he must have taken as a diminutive young cowhand down the bar when, one way or another, the harmless-looking squirt shot him dead as a turd in a milk bucket."

He let that sink in before he added, "They call the young squirt Billy the Kid. He's still out there, walking soft and smiling friendly as ever, and now and then, some bigger kid makes the mistake of messing with him."

Skane nodded soberly and said, "I've heard-tell of Billy the Kid. I understand he's the quickest draw in the West."

Longarm snorted and declared, "I can't think of a recorded case of the Kid beating anybody to the draw. I just tried to explain he's so dangerous because he's a killer who looks harmless. Weren't you paying attention to me, damn it?"

"Sure," Skane said. "You said to watch out for quiet little guys down at the far end of the bar. I could have told you that. That Irishman last night started up with me. What kind of an asshole without a gun of his own sticks his chest out at a man packing his six-gun in a tied-down rig?"

"An asshole, I reckon," Longarm conceded, before adding, "You'd best not go to the saloon this evening. I want you to shack up with that same whore or a prettier one whilst I scout the saloon in a less flamboyant way. You may have done right. You may have left a lasting impression we don't have to worry about. If your dancing partner shows up with more of the same, it might be time to head on down to Pot Luck."

"I don't want nobody saying I was run out of any town," Skane growled.

Longarm said, "When you leave before anybody can tell you to leave they can't say they ran you out of town. Didn't you know that was why old John Wesley Hardin moved around so much?"

Skane grinned like a kid stealing apples and said, "Hot damn, I'd sure like to have folk comparing me to John

Wesley Hardin! Where is our Texas answer to Wild Bill Hickok these days, pard?"

Longarm said, "Texas State Prison at Huntsville. Texas Ranger captain called Armstrong tracked him all the way to Alabama, and Texas gave him twenty-five at hard. You're supposed to admire famous *lawmen*, not the famous *outlaws* like Billy the Kid and Wes Hardin, Buck."

Skane pointed out that few lawmen seemed to rack up the scores of victims most famous outlaws seemed to manage.

Longarm let it go. Life was too short to waste time arguing with a woman, a boss or a born fool.

After sundown, back in town on that same porch, Longarm told Hazel he had to step over to the saloon a spell before he took her up the road for more soda pop.

She said, "You never shaved, like I asked. When I saw you hadn't at breakfast or at dinner I was hoping you meant to get all smooth and kissy for our . . . evening stroll. But you're commencing to look like a hobo and you say you're going to that *saloon*?"

He said, "On business. Only on business. You know I'd rather drink soda pop with you and I mean to, soon as I can get back to you no later than, say, ten?"

"You expect me to mope around out here as late as that?" she demanded, adding, "Who's this other person you have such important business with? Is she pretty?"

Longarm truthfully replied, "I understand she's the bully of the town and wears pants. My pard, Buck, had words with him last night whiles you and me were . . . sipping soda pop. I want to make sure it's over."

She said, "Oh, dear, you must be talking about Dinty Donovan! Is that why you've been letting your chin whiskers grow, trying to look tougher, Canada?"

He allowed it might be something like that. She laughed and said men were such boys and she expected him back no later than ten.

He promised he'd try and headed on over in the gathering dusk to find the saloon expectantly crowded with the mirror behind the bar put away and the wagon-wheel oil chandelier taken down. Longarm hadn't more than glanced in up until then. So he couldn't say whether the sawdust on the floor was spread deeper than usual. It sure was deep in any case.

Longarm quietly made his way to one end of the bar and waited in silence for the barkeep to notice him. Once the barkeep had, Longarm ordered a schooner of draft and paid up front, leaving his change on the zinc top of the bar. The best way for a stranger to occasion a lull in the conversation was to start asking questions in a strange bar. On the other hand, after they got used to your silent presence the regulars tended to forget you were there.

The conversation, such as he could make out, seemed to involve the topic of Free Silver, with most agreeing the infernal government had no call to set the market price of any infernal metal.

An older gent with a silver mustache and a brass star on his vest bellied up beside Longarm to declare, "I would be Constable Vandemeer and I was wondering where your pard Mr. Skane was, Mr. Cooper."

Longarm said, "I advised him it might be best if he didn't show up this evening, Constable. I was hoping things had blown over, but I see they ain't?"

Vandemeer said, "You don't rawhide the bully of a town with a loaded pissoliver and then let him walk away *alive*. I have warned Dinty Donovan I'll have no bloodshed here in Jimtown. In return for his promise to be good tonight, I have promised him Buck Skane won't be in town more than twenty-four hours."

He let that sink in and sounded serious as he calmly went on, "Dinty knows I am a man of my word. I hope you believe that. Because if your pissoliver-waving pal is still in town this time tomorrow night, he may never see another sunrise. Do we understand one another, Mr. Cooper?"

Longarm sipped some suds before he soberly replied, "We do if you let me get old Buck out of town my way, Constable. As we have both observed, old Buck's inclined to get excited when it looks as if somebody is out to rawhide him. I can likely get him to come along as I head on down to a new strike I've heard about in a place called Pot Luck. If he hears one word about somebody bragging on running him out of town, he's likely to want to stay and fight it out."

"He could wind up dead. You could both wind up dead," said the older lawman.

"No saying who might wind up dead when bullets commence flying all about," said Longarm, nodding. "Let me do her my way and the both of 'em will get to brag on coming out on top."

"Get Skane out of town before another sundown and we got us a deal," Vandemeer said. "Have you been up this way before, Mr. Cooper?"

Longarm answered honestly enough, "More than once, albeit this is the first time we've talked about it. I've been here and I've been yonder in this high country. I ain't *wanted* nowhere, if that's what you want to know."

The older lawman said, "It was. As we've been talking I've been running your somehow familiar features through my wanted fliers and that ain't it. Reckon I've just got used to you passing through. I hope I don't see you no more for a spell."

Longarm said, "I was figuring on noon tomorrow. Need to buy us a buckboard, find us some good mules and stock up on supplies before we head on down to Pot Luck. Being it's a new strike, prices down yonder will be through the roof and I notice the second-growth timber's grown thicker than walking sticks up this way."

The man who lived there said, "Things have settled down tolerable here in Jimtown. That's why I aim to keep things that way. I understand old Hiram Ballard has a buckboard that still rolls for sale. Don't buy mules off anybody but Kimoho Page at the west end of town. He's not as well situated as some but he's honest, for a breed."

He thought and shrugged. "Mining supplies are still fixing to cost you in mining country. Any claim producing color can afford to pay top dollar for their dynamite and blasting caps. Hard-rock miners employed in a mine can afford to pay dear for food and clothing. Hard-rock miners who don't have jobs can't afford to live around here."

Longarm allowed he'd been through the high country before, finished his beer and got back to the boarding house well before ten. So he had to wait on the porch until Hazel came down around nine-thirty.

On their way up the road for some soda pop, Hazel swung him around in a pool of thick shadow to kiss him. Once she had, she demanded they go on back to the boarding house so's he could shave, saying, "I don't mind your mustache, darling. It feels silky and tickles. But your blue jowels feel like emery paper and, damn it, I like to kiss when I fornicate!"

He said, "So do I. But you will just have to put up with my stubble 'til it smooths out, some. Shaving nicks are dangerous working down in muggy mine shaft where the air ain't pure and Lord knows who's been hawking and spitting."

She sighed, "Oh, you're so romantic. I've a good mind to say good night here and now, but whilst the *spirit* is annoyed with you the *flesh* has been itching since suppertime and you know that, don't you, you brute?"

He said, "Ain't trying to brutalize nobody. Told you the way things have to be. You want to go back to the house, now?"

She pouted she hadn't had her soda pop yet. So they went on to the general store and then went on some more, sipping soda through straws as the timber got taller to either side. Aspen made piss-poor firewood and once a mining camp was making money, it hauled in coal and proper kindling from the nearest railhead.

Seeing his stubble had gotten to where it was tormenting *him* and knowing it would be their last time out in the timber together, Longarm tried to make it up to her with some serious long donging and she got so excited she didn't seem to mind his whiskers after all.

He didn't tell her it would be their last night in the tall timber. He knew that of all the ways to leave a lover, nothing beat just leaving and letting them figure out you were gone. It saved a heap of wear and tear on the gal when she didn't have to carry on the way late Victorian maidens were expected to.

So next morning after a prim and proper but sort of disgusting breakfast of oatmeal sweetened with black-jack molasses, Longarm took Buchanan T. aside and instructed him on how to look as if he was bargaining for shit. Between them they managed to leave town before noon aboard a lightly loaded sun-silvered buckboard behind two middle-aged mules that still had a few miles left in them.

Longarm explained it made more sense to travel light most of the way and pick up more flour, canned goods and such as needed. For there was no call to freight a can of pork and beans or tomato preserves for days before you ever opened them.

Following mountain roads and wagon traces in a generally south-by-southwest direction, they rolled into Pot Luck four days later, along about sundown. Skane huffed and puffed them into a rickety structure advertising itself as a hotel. The proprietor offered to stable the mules and store the buckboard in a padlocked shed for a few dollars more a week after Skane explained they needed a place to stay in town whilst they prospected the hills nearby.

Alone upstairs, old Buck blushed like a bride when Longarm told him he'd done good and added, "Saves us a lot of trouble if we were to buy a bottomed-out claim, work her a spell and let folk get used to us before we strike some color."

Skane frowned and asked, "How in thunder might you strike color in a worthless bottomed-out claim, pard?"

Longarm said to let him worry about that and suggested they get some sleep. When Skane allowed it was still early and the saloons were just cranking up for the night, Longarm said, "I just now said we want to let folk get used to us being here before we did or said all that much. With any luck nobody that matters knows we're here yet."

He was wrong, of course. Not far away, since the camp was so small, a man who didn't miss much was asking the town law about those strangers who'd been in his town for over an hour, God damn it.

The town law said, "Don't get your bowels in an uproar, boss. I told you I'd put out feelers by wire and I did. Buck Skane and his quieter sidekick left Jimtown in Boulder County last Friday. Old Pete Vandemeer ran Skane out for getting into a fight over some gal up yonder. When our pals up yonder asked him, the constable said the blond bully and his more bashful *segundo* have been prospecting up here in the high country a spell. Said they'd tried up around Jimtown and hadn't had no luck before Skane got in trouble over that gal. Could we talk about that Denver gent who's vanished from his local claim, now? Kin in Denver keep asking and don't you think we ought to tell them *something*?"

Chapter 5

As rattletrapped and jury-rigged as their hotel was, Buck and Longarm were served flapjacks for breakfast under sorghum syrup with Arbuckle brand coffee and bacon only two bits extra if you wanted it. Up to the ordering of fancy extras, the meals were on the American plan and were included in the price of the rooms. Two dollars a day in such a boomtown, take it or leave it.

The spanking new camp on the west slope of the Front Range was a confusion of painted canvas and raw lumber that would likely never wind up with brick walls and sandstone walks. Like the older and more substantial Jimtown to the north, Pot Luck's modest business district was sprung along one main steet with even more primitive housing scattered like chaff across a network of footpaths to either side. There was no running stream supporting placer operations. Such water as there was came from wells, with only the ones upslope of the shit houses halfway safe to drink without considerable boiling. Like the original claim the settlement was named for, the few other places men had spotted color, or thought they had, were mostly strung along a reef of granite outcropped in line of, but downgrade from, the north-south contour line the one main street followed like a drunk doing his best. Since a discouraging amount of what looked like color turned out to be mica or pyrites, there were dozens of try holes. Shafts sunk as dreams deep or shallow, for every producing claim. You could tell a try hole from a mine at a glance because it was only after a try hole started to yield something better than pure rock that you saw tram rails, piles of crushed tailings and such around the entrance. Only small mines following a modest vein were still drilled, blasted and mucked by hand this late in the game. So you saw the tram cable tipples, air hoses leading from steam-powered pump houses to the jack-hammering Burleigh drills and such. So far, those few claims producing wealth instead of heartbreaking effort around Pot Luck were still being worked the old-fashioned way. The old joke about it taking a gold mine to operate a silver mine was only funny the first time you heard it. But even extracting ore by coolie labor paid off slow but sure as long as there was enough color in a ton of muck to pay more than the cost of somehow getting it to and through the smelter.

They bitched and moaned, but hard-rock miners could be hired at three dollars a shift and ore that assayed at less than a dollar a ton wasn't worth drilling for.

The gaping mouth of many an abandoned try hole along that granite reef testified to granite that didn't contain a dollar's worth of color to the ton.

As he and Buck strode around the new field, avoiding conversation with the few locals they met up with along the footpaths, Longarm coached his nominal senior partner on what he was supposed to say the following day. It took a heap of coaching because old Buck seemed a slow learner you had to repeat things to. Longarm would have held off the first day in any case. A newcomer who even appeared interested in a particular place the first day was a man who'd shown up knowing something.

That night they both went to the biggest combined bordello and saloon in town, which wasn't saying much. They called the place the Crystal Palace, even though it had been constructed of two-by-fours and siding of green knotty pine. Longarm had decided it was best to tag along and see how much trouble he might head off before it happened. He chose the inside seat of a corner table and warned Skane not to turn and cast any inviting glances over his shoulder as they shared a scuttle of beer and a bowl of popcorn.

They were still approached more than once and the beefy blond Skane did all the talking, as instructed earlier by his silent partner.

It wasn't so tough that first night, since all Skane had to say was that they'd just got there and were still looking. It was safe for him to add in as quiet a brag as he could manage that he had himself a grand notion about that reef others had drilled into in vain. Longarm idly wondered if the Texican knew what he was talking about as he said he'd noticed how all that real money had been made in nearby Leadville by more serious investors who'd busted through the crust of gold quartz into tons of lower-grade but inexhaustable loads of softer chlorides way down deep.

As a dreamer who'd long thirsted for fame and fortune, Skane had been enthralled by and quickly memorized the roll of the dice that had made a rich man out of Silver Dollar Tabor.

It was a well-known yarn and more than one curious local left to go take a leak or something before the enthusiastic Skane could finish the tale of the knavish Chicken Bill Lovell diddling old Hod Tabor with a forty-foot try hole he'd salted with ore he'd stolen from Tabor's own Little Pittsburgh lode. But if pressed, old Buck was willing to just explain to the smoke-filled air across the table, "You see, Hod Tabor was more of a grocery-store man than a prospector. He'd only got started by grubstaking real prospectors with supplies on credit in exchange for shares in anything they might find. So Chicken Bill was still bragging to his drinking pals about how slick he'd suckered the fool Scotchman when Tabor, not knowing no better, had his hired hand sink the try hole another eight feet through pure country rock into high-grade chrisolite paying a hundred thousand a month for the next two years! Ain't that a bitch?"

A thirsty-looking individual offering to hammer a star drill for a dollar a day agreed a heap of try holes had likely been abandoned all too soon but called old Buck a cheapskate when he was told any man who could pay others to drill before he hit pay dirt was not a *prospector* but a fat cat *investor*. As the old barfly got up to leave, Skane hurled after him, "Silver Dollar Tabor had his Little Pittsburgh supporting him and his family in style when he turned the tables on Chicken Bill with other men's sweat. Now he's so rich without working he gets to while away his time with a private bagpipe band and a bodacious mistress too young for his son Nate to mess with! Ain't that a bitch?"

After that nobody came to their table for a spell. Buchanan T. Skane had that effect on others once they saw he wasn't buying anything they were selling.

When he felt safe to do so, Skane asked Longarm how he was doing.

Longarm said, "Not bad. We've established we're in the market for a not-too-deep abandoned try hole. Ought to be safe to buy one out in a day or so."

Skane asked, "How come you have to *buy* a hole in the ground nobody else seems to want?"

Longarm explained, "Once you hit pay dirt, that's when the one with the original notion recalls he never surrendered clear title and you pay him off or the lawyers wind up making more money out of the hole than anybody else."

Skane asked, "Can't you look it up before you start? Ain't the one who sank the try hole expected to fill out papers and such?"

Longarm sipped some suds, sighed and said, "Some do.

40

Some don't. Even those who can read the complexicated rules and regulations might save on the filing fees by waiting until they strike color before filing a claim. Many an illiterate prospector's struck, worked and abandoned a placer or pocket of high grade without anyone else ever bein' the wiser. You hear tales of lost or secret gold mines all across the country. Some of 'em are likely true. But prior records are neither hither nor yon. Claim jumpers are by definition pests who wait for somebody else to strike color before they recall they were there first. It's tougher to deny anybody was there before you when you're standing in a hole dug by somebody else."

"Then why don't we just start our own hole, somewhere nobody's been digging before?" asked the Texican.

Longarm said, "Two reasons. It takes longer to produce a substantial looking hole in the ground, starting from scratch, and there's no way to be sure some pest won't produce an assay report showing he already poked about there, before you make certain."

"So how do you make certain?" asked Skane.

Longarm said, "Title search. You retain a local lawyer to go through the local records and find you a claim that was filed on preliminary but abandoned before the full fees on a proven claim were paid."

He sipped more suds and explained, "It's like that Homestead Act. You prove title to your claim a step at a time with a lawyer holding your little hand so you don't get lost. That's how come they have as many lawyers as whores up this way. I know what Billy Vail said about letting you do all the talking. But a junior partner asking sensible questions is likely to leave less of a wake through shark-infested waters than a gent who'd obviously never filed a mining claim before, no offense. So, come morning, you'd best sleep late whilst I quietly retain us a local mouthpiece."

Old Buck beamed expansively and decided he'd best

find some action to tire himself out if he meant to sleep late. He said, "I've been trying to make up my mind about that poker game in the opposite corner or that black-headed gal in the red fandango outfit, smiling at me so lonesome from the end of the bar. I can tell she sort of likes me."

Longarm was too polite to speculate on why the lady of the evening in red seemed so lonesome in a saloon full of mining men. He said, "I reckon she can't possibly screw you out of more money than that tinhorn with the green eye shade in yonder corner. But take it easy on the pocket jingle I gave you coming in this morning. When the field expenses we started out with are gone they're gone. I doubt Billy will send more if I was to take the chance of wiring for it."

Buchanan T. drained the stein he'd been working on and rose to head over to the gal, who, now that Longarm studied on her, seemed to be giving the eye to the both of them.

He looked away and replenished his own stein from the bigger scuttle.

He meant to nurse what was left as he sat alone in his corner, observing the local scene like a bug student studying one of those ant farms with his magnifying glass. It sure beat all how ants, and regulars in a saloon, could go on waving their feelers at one another without being aware they might be being watched. He suspected he was the only one there watching that scrawny whore with the shoe blacking in her hair hauling old Buck up those stairs behind the bar.

He felt less smug about his cloak of invisibility a few minutes later when an older and shorter cuss in an undertaker's suit, a summer straw hat and his own schooner of beer sat down across from him, uninvited, to ask, "Mind if I join you, Mr. Cooper?"

Longarm smiled thinly and resisted the opening to be snotty. The smaller local wonder settled in with his beer to say, "I saw you and your sidekick poking around along the reef earlier. You're the one who has the final say, right?"

To which Longarm could only reply, "You seem a man of snap judgments, Mr. . . . ?"

The stranger said, "Zip Finny is the name and mining supplies would be my game. I can't afford to miss much, extending credit on shares in the pot at the end of the rainbow. I take it you boys were looking for a shortcut to China, or, least ways, through that low-grade granite and down into softer and richer chlorides?"

Longarm sipped some suds and decided, "Could be. Might you have such a shortcut to China in mind?"

Finny nodded and said, "Couple of boys I thought better of drilled and blasted nigh sixty feet. More than halfway through that quartz-veined granite pretending to be possible pay dirt. Then they up and departed like thieves in the night, abandoning their claim and stiffing me for better than a thousand dollars, leaving me holding a hole in the ground I hope you might be interested in."

Longarm asked, "What sort of *paper* are you holding, Mr. Finny?"

The supply man who'd grubstaked the fly-by-nights said, "Outstanding debt with their claim as security. I don't extend credit unless there's a claim on file with the Bureau of Mines. Don't worry about the title search. My lawyer's shuffled such papers for me in the past. We can have that sixty-foot try hole rock solid in your names within forty-eight hours and you can start drilling come tomorrow morning if you like. So how do you like it so far?"

Longarm said, "I like it a hundred dollars worth. Cash on the barrel head when you produce the deed and quitclaim."

Zip Finny gasped, "Sweet Jesus, the legal fees will set me back over a hundred dollars. How am I supposed to go for a deal like that?"

Longarm shrugged and said, "For openers you retain a lawyer who'll do the routine paperwork for five. We're

43

talking about a law clerk making out fresh forms without adult supervision."

Finny said, "Just the same, you're asking me to wind up with less than ten cents on the damned dollar, Mr. Cooper."

Longarm said, "That's ten cents more on the dollar than nothing. How often might you sell a claim abandoned as worthless? Me and old Buck can hire a crew to dig us a new hole somewhere else along that reef for three dollars a day and with any luck they might strike color on their way to China, right?"

Zip Finny swore he'd never surrender such a swell hole in the ground for less than five hundred, and in the end they settled for two, with the legal fees coming out of Finny's pocket provided the team of Buchanan and Cooper put up fifty in interest money.

Longarm snapped a twenty-dollar double eagle on the table between them as he said, "Take it or leave it. I don't know you all that well, either. You'll get the rest when you produce unencumbered possession, and like the Indian chief said, I have spoken."

Zip Finny made the gold coin vanish with a rude remark about only just now learning Cooper was a Scotch name and promising to have the transfer papers and the more important quitclaim drawn up by the coming noon. It was as important to get that quitclaim as a deed to the claim because so many pests who sold mining property free and clear suddenly remembered a share or more they'd never surrendered when or if somebody found color they figured it was only fair to share.

They shook on it and the older man scuttled off with Longarm's double eagle, leaving Longarm to idly wonder if he'd ever see the son of a bitch again. It was a chance he'd felt worth taking. Working a sixty-foot try hole, out of the sight of curious eyes, opened opportunities that would not have been there, starting from scratch on the surface. They had to get down into the reef a ways before anybody was going to believe they'd stumbled over pay dirt.

He sipped more suds and consulted his pocket watch as he waited for old Buck to get down with that black-headed gal upstairs. He knew that no matter how romantic old Buck felt, no professional was about to give much more time up yonder. He had to tell his senior partner what they'd just done and see if he could get the boisterous Texican bedded safely down for the night. There was no telling what Skane might let slip in the course of a likkered up night on the town, left to his own devices.

Longarm had no way of knowing the scrawny black-headed whore had been instructed to offer more than usual in the way of pillow talk to a new boy in town.

Skilled in the art of pumping customers at both ends, she'd already needled him about striking her as a sweet but mighty green hard-rock miner, after catching him in a couple of green remarks on the subject.

So as he felt her withered tit and one of her scrawny limbs hooked over his bare gut, Buchanan T. Skane confided, "A lot you know. I may not know as much as some of your other boyfriends about the mining game, but that's only because I'm an experienced lawman, up this way on this secret mission, see?"

She reached down to take his limp manhood in hand as she purred like a kitten and asked what sort of a secret mission they might be talking about.

Buchanan T. smiled smugly and said, "That's for me to know and you to just wonder. What kind of a secret mission would it be if I informed you all about it?"

"Not very secret," she agreed, trying to keep a straight face.

Chapter 6

Under federal legislation of the day, a homestead claim consisted of a quarter section of 160 acres, a section being a square mile. Preliminary mineral claims were much smaller with way fewer strings attached. You didn't have to reside on them or hold them for five years before you could sell or transfer title. The standard placer claim was a hundred square feet, most often with the streambed being worked filling half of it. Surface claims to an underground lode were staked out fifty feet wide and a hundred feet long, or about the size of a building lot on a fashionable residential street in Denver. What they called the rule of apex gave a mining claim holder the right to follow any lode struck near the surface inside the bounds of his claim most anywhere down yonder, leading to some interesting discussions involving dynamite and steam hoses down yonder on occasion.

The government allowed you to buy unclaimed land around your primary claim at five dollars an acre if you felt the need to expand into, say, a company town. It was considered more prudent to hit pay dirt first, albeit some canny stockmen with sharp lawyers had already dispensed with the red tape of claiming their home spreads under the

Homested Act in favor of filing a mineral claim on, say, mighty low-grade ore spread out all around, paying five dollars an acre, lest the government feel cheated.

It had already been proven in court that there was *some* gold, silver or whatever in most every granite boulder in the Rocky Mountains, since granite, after cooling and setting like fudge for millions of years, was mostly feldspar, silica and such with microscopic particles of every other mineral from aluminum to zinc scattered through it like stars in a sky of stone.

This thin pudding of the original bedrock had resulted in way more interesting geology once Mother Nature had kneaded the gray makings of her mountains like bread dough for millions more years. Volcanic magma and all sorts of god-awful steaming brews of acid and alkaline waters were stirred together under impossible pressure to form ore bodies of every shape man could imagine, along with some he couldn't where there was no way to look without drilling and blasting into them the hard-rock way.

The try hole Longarm and Buck had taken title to by the next afternoon occupied an ever steepening site consisting of thirty by fifty feet of packed earth and seventy by fifty feet of that confusing granite outcrop, with the try hole a six-by-six-foot unbraced adit leading into what looked more like a rabbit hole with delusions of grandeur than a gold mine. It slanted into the reef at a twelve-degree grade. Five muddy, splintered one-inch planks had been laid single file from the adit to a churned up muddy work area near the vertical face not really a full sixty feet from fresh air but close enough for Longarm's purposes. The partnership who'd skipped out on its local bills had left with their lamps, picks and shovels, but had abandoned a wheelbarrow as too awkward to abscond with, bless their souls.

Turning to the confused senior partner who'd followed him to the face in an uncomfortable stoop, Longarm said, "It's too late in the day to do much down here. But we can save on outrageous hotel rates if we haul our possibles out here and set up camp."

Skane complained, "Checkout time is after noon. So we are stuck for the rest of today, anyhow, and rate a fair supper on the American plan."

Longarm said, "I noticed. We'll haul our buckboard out here and pitch our tent for all the world to see right after supper. One of us has to stay and guard our supplies. One of us has to lead the mules back to town and leave 'em in a livery for now. That may as well be you, and as long as you have to go to town where a hotel room will still be at your disposal, I don't care if you want to get screwed, blewed and tattooed as long as you don't get in any *fights*. I got chores best done under cover of darkness to occupy my mind tonight. Drilling into granite can get tedious when you know what you're about with a sledge and star drill. I'm out of practice and I mostly held the drill whilst making sure I wanted to herd cows instead of moil for gold out this way, after the war."

Skane held the one lantern they were sharing up to the rough wall of elephant-gray granite with lard-colored quartz to ask, "Do you reckon there *could* be any color in all this hard rock?"

"The old boys who drilled this deep into her must not have noticed much," Longarm said. "They sure left a lot of tailings piled up outside. They'd have hauled more to the stamping mill if it had assayed worth the bother."

Skane sighed and said, "Wouldn't it be a pisser if we were to persist our way into a bonanza. I've always wanted to be rich. Ain't you?"

Longarm chuckled dryly and said, "Stick with me and I'll show you how."

Skane blinked at him and said, "I don't get it. Are you saying you know something the boys who gave up on this hole missed? What was all that shit about chloroform you and Zip Finny were talking about earlier?"

Longarm said, "Chloride was the word you were grop-
ing for. There's this hellacious mix of acids called *aqua regia* that dissolves gold and all the other metals as it bubbles
through the bowels of this earth, way down deep. As it
pools in cavities closer to the surface and the water boils
away in dirt-filled cavities, metallic salts called chlorides
as in hydrochloric acid are left behind. I suspect Zip Finny
was out to sell us a worthless claim. This reef is original
bedrock, possibly folded over with surface deposits of
sands and clays during the churning that produced such
rocky mountains. It's just as likely this granite goes down
all the way to the elephant standing on a turtle."

He pointed up the slope toward the western sky as he
added, "I mean to strike us some gold quartz after we've
pretended to work this claim a few days. Let's get on back
to town. Trim that lamp and leave it in yon corner."

Skane did as he was told and scrambled after Longarm
with both their heads bent lower. As they blinked out into
the afternoon sunlight, Skane gasped, "What are you talking about? Nobody can strike color on demand like a fucking magician!"

Longarm lit a cheroot as he regained his bearings, saying, "Sure they can, with a little stage magic. This magical
gal I used to know says it's all in what she called misdirection. It ain't what you do. It's what you get the audience to
think you're doing whilst you're doing something else."

As he gazed about, sizing up his likely audience, he saw
nobody on the footpath up-slope could make out the adit or
much of what might be going on in the flat patch west of it.
The nearest claim to the south lay seventy-five yards along
the reef. Finny said he'd grubstaked the one old loner
working that one. Longarm saw no signs of activity over
yonder. So the claim holder was in town or down his try
hole a ways.

A covered wagon blocked most of his view into the site
of the claim to their north, more like 150 yards on up the

reef with a pathetic shallow attempt at a try hole between. It was easy to get discouraged, drilling into granite grain by grain with a star drill and a nine-pound sledge that didn't get any lighter as you swung it by the hour.

Finny had allowed a dude he didn't know much about was working that claim with his wife and kids keeping him company. Finny had said that was all he knew about that claim. As Longarm gazed north he saw a little girl with a sand bucket digging her own gold mine on the shady side of their wagon. So Finny had had that part right, at least. It made for an interesting contrast, with their neighbor to the south likely jerking off betwixt visits to the Crystal Palace and their neighbor to the north living sort of like a gypsy family man in residence.

As they walked the short distance back to town, old Buck pestered him about this mysterious misdirection shit. Longarm suggested they let him worry about it. Old Buck was turning out as loose a cannon as he'd feared and the less he really knew the less he could blab about. Longarm would have called their mission off then and there if he'd known how much the Texas windbag had already spilled. Longarm only had him down as a fool, not a *damned* fool.

Once in town they hitched the mules to their buckboard to do a little shopping down to the south end, where the merchants had an easier haul to and from the narrow-gauge line cutting east and west to the south of Pot Luck.

Longarm had bought most of the supplies they'd needed up in Jimtown where prices were less *loco en la cabeza*. But nobody in his right mind trucked dynamite better than a hundred miles on the bed of a buckboard. The only springs to a buckboard were under the seat. Everything else on the flatbed got bucked and bounced on unsprung planking.

Dynamite came packed in sawdust and its invention had made Mr. Nobel of Sweden so rich because it could take a certain amount of rough handling before you were ready to set it off. But a hundred miles worth of thumps and bumps were best avoided, where possible. So Longarm stopped by Zip Finny's general store to pick them up a case.

Old Finny offered them a price on sixty percent Hercules brand if they cared to buy a dozen cases at a time. But Longarm said, "Not hardly. One case going off at a time in our vicinity could be injurious to our health. We figure on having no more than a day's worth of blasting on hand at a time if it's all the same with you."

Old Zip shrugged and said, "Suit yourself. I got close to a hundred cases out back and it ain't gone off on me yet."

Longarm said, "It likely won't. But better you than us, no offense."

He paid with a federal silver certificate. He'd slipped that slyly out of the money belt he was using as his gun belt. He'd felt no call to tell old Buck where their travel expenses seemed to arrive from. Old Buck had never asked. For a man who hungered so for fame and fortune, Old Buck seemed to take little interest in such tedious details. Longarm suspected few hound dogs worried about where the dog food you fed 'em came from, as long as you kept feeding 'em.

Back at their claim, Skane helped Longarm set up their tent and the army cots Longarm had picked up at a bargain in Jimtown. Then he led the team back to town, offering to come back and spell Longarm if Longarm wanted to have that supper they still owed him at their hotel. He grinned like a kid let loose from school when Longarm told him not to bother.

Longarm said he'd fix himself some canned beans and put a coffeepot on their night fire. But that wasn't what he was concerned about. What he was concerned about was anybody reading over his shoulder as he whipped up a fairy tale.

He puttered around their campsite, with the buckboard

naturally in the space betwixt the adit and the tent, leaving barely enough room for a night fire in the corner of their claim. As he did so, he noticed the way bigger covered wagon to the north was parked with one end close to the reef. But it seemed out of line from the adit if a blast went off premature, or into a hot spring. So maybe the family man up that way knew what he was about.

Longarm took his time building their night fire and wound up lazing by the same, eating beans, as the sun went down. He noticed his neighbors north and south came into view along the western edges of their claims to admire the same sunset. Folk were funny that way.

Sometimes you'd see dogs, cats and other livestock staring into the sunset at the end of another day, as if they'd never seen one all the other days of their lives. Birds seemed to notice, too. Gray jays and cross beaks all around were calling fit to bust after the setting sun.

The old-timer and his kid helper to their south seemed not to notice Longarm's friendly wave as he stood there like a bean pole. When Longarm swung around casual, he saw those two little kids and their nondescript mom, in a sunbonnet and Mother Hubbard of matching blue-checked calico, had their own eyes on that suspiciously acting sun. Their pa wasn't present. He was likely in town. Nobody drilled granite when there was a sundown to be seen just outside.

Longarm's only complaint with that particular one was that it seemed to be taking so long. He wanted it dark before he stirred from his lazy reclining pose by an after-supper fire.

After what only felt like a million years, the stars started coming out and Longarm rose to stroll slowly into the try hole, knowing sudden movements drew attention, even in tricky light.

He didn't light his lamp as he felt his way to the abandoned wheelbarrow and rolled it up the end-to-end planks.

Out by the tailing pile, he let it set a spell as he fetched some dynamite from the buckboard bed to cap, fuse and tote down the try hole. There he lined them up neatly against the granite face along one long fuse.

Then he went out and, working quietly with a mucking spade from the buckboard, filled the wheelbarrow with disappointing shit that had already been mucked by those earlier dreamers. He wheeled the worthless shattered rock back down where it had come from and spread it gently and did it some more until he had his dynamite buried under a couple of tons of what could have been described as pointless effort if Longarm hadn't had some misdirection in mind.

Over in Pot Luck, as Buchanan T. was trying to parley the few dollars his nominal junior partner had doled out into pocket jingle. He figured if he won he could afford somebody more suited to his station than old Greek Gloria whilst, if he got cleaned out again, he'd just have to ask good old Longarm for more.

Upstairs, in another part of Pot Luck, the town marshal, who'd been appointed by the city council, was reporting in full to the man he took his orders from: a self-effacing soul who admired hell out of the late Niccolo Machiavelli and prefered to be called Mr. Prince by the very few in town who knew he existed.

As they chatted in an unlit office closed for the night, the town law said, "What that Texas windbag told Greek Gloria last night was true in the way that old lime-juicer, calling himself the one true and authentic Deadwood Dick, claimed he really worked in a saloon up yonder a few years back."

"I never asked you to check out Richard Clarke or those dime novels about a Deadwood Dick written by Edward Wheeler," Mr. Prince said. "You were asked to check out that towheaded Texan who claims to be a lawman on a secret mission, Marshal Ellison."

Ellison said, "I did. Like I told you, I know lawmen all over this country. The one calling hisself Buchanan T. Skane answers to the name and unusual description on file with the Texas Rangers. Skane applied for a ranger badge a spell back. He couldn't pass the written entrance exam. He applied to be a federal deputy in San Antone and they told him not to be silly. He wrangled a job as a county brand inspector down by the border and told all the gals in town he was a range detective. After he lost that job he worked for a time as a turnkey in the Val Verde County Jail. He couldn't seem to understand it was the prisoners in the back that were supposed to sleep at night with him on guard. Buchanan T. Skane adds up, in sum, to one of them Irishmen who deliver bread all day but let it be known after dark in a public house that they're captains in the local Fenian battalion."

Mr. Prince made a wry face in the dark and asked, "What about his quieter sidekick, the one called Canada?"

Marshal Ellison said, "He ain't from Texas. Like I told you, they know him up around Jimtown as just a quiet cuss who can't be all that smart if he's out to work that worthless claim with that famous Texas terror, Buchanan T. Skane."

"Keep an eye on them, anyway," said Mr. Prince, adding in a soft purr, "I worry about dumb assholes. You can never be sure what they'll do next."

Chapter 7

What Longarm was doing next, alone in the tent by lamplight, involved more dynamite, some of that gold leaf from Denver and other items he'd picked up in Jimtown and didn't want anyone in Pot Luck to know about.

After wrapping one to three tissue-thin sheets of gold leaf around a stick of greasy-feeling Hercules sixty percent, Longarm brushed library paste on paper close to the same color as the dynamite sticks and wrapped it around the sticks and over the gold leaf.

Then he broke out the kid's rubber stamp kit he'd bought in a toy store. Earlier, he'd set the rubber type in the slotted wood stamp provided to read HERCULES 60%, and if neither the size nor the font of the lettering matched on close examination, who was going to examine his salted sticks worth mention? The game was up as soon as anyone *suspected* there might be a thing irregular about those sticks of dynamite.

Fortunately the dynamite logo and the stamp pad that came with the kid's kit were close to the same shade of red. As he was wiping dirt into the last doctored stick, Longarm nearly dropped the dynamite as he heard a small voice declare, "I'm Willie Mae and I'm almost five."

55

Longarm turned on the cot to soberly inform the child in the flour-sack night shift and straw-colored hair set in pigtails, "I'm neither. How did you get in here, sis?"

He already knew where she'd come from. He'd watched her playing up by that covered wagon earlier.

Willie Mae pointed to the slit of the shut but not buttoned tent falp she'd come through to say, "I saw you were up doing something in here so I came in to see what you were doing. What are you doing, Mister?"

Knowing better than to tell any woman to keep a secret, Longarm put the last stick he'd doctored in with the others as he said, "I was putting things away and now I'm all finished. Do your folk know you're this far from you own camp, Willie Mae?"

She shrugged and said, "I reckon. Why do you keep dynamite under your cot, Mister? My daddy keeps his in a hole in the ground."

A distant she-male voice was calling out, sort of anquished, "Willie Mae! Where are you?"

Longarm rose to duck past the child, step out of the tent and call back. "She's over this way, ma'am. No harm done. Just curious, I reckon, and here we come!"

He held out a hand to say, "Let's go, sis. You got your folk worried and we'd best get you home now."

Willie Mae put a trusting hand in his and he decided to let her folk warn her about dirty old men as he headed with her toward the covered wagon outlined by its own night fire. A figure he recognized as the wayward kid's ma was coming to meet them, fast, with the light behind her outlining her long lean legs through her own thin nightgown. They looked swell. Longarm told himself to think purer thoughts. A man who even thought about the legs of a neighbor's woman was one who'd lost interest in reaching old age. As a lawman, Longarm knew how many fools died young, thinking impure thoughts about their neighbor's women.

It got even harder to think pure as the worried young matron joined them on the dirt path. Her auburn hair was down for the night and the kindly light from the night fire behind Longarm likely softened her already soft features in a sort of magical way.

She said, "I'm so sorry, sir. I've told both the kids to stay on our claim, but . . ."

"They're kids," Longarm pointed out with a knowing smile, adding, "I answer to Canada Cooper and my partner, the big blond cuss you may have noticed earlier would be Buchanan or Buck Skane. He don't eat little girls, neither, as far as I know."

Willie Mae said, "Mr. Growly Bug, the mean old man who has the claim on the other side of yours, says he's fixing to bite my toes off if I visit him again."

Her mother said, "I believe he said his name was Goldberg when he brought her back to us. I'm afraid she didn't believe him."

Longarm nodded and said, "I never advise nobody on joining the army, marrying up or raising their own kids, ma'am. According to many married-up friends, nothing seems to work, anyhow."

They both chuckled. Then she said, "I'd be Nell Fordham and where are my manners? When I saw you and your friend moving in earlier I thought about coming down your way with a pie. But I'm afraid I . . . haven't been baking. My man's been gone longer than expected and we're running a bit low on flour. But why don't you join us up the line for some coffee, at least? We've still got plenty of coffee."

So Longarm walked the two of them up the reef, with Willie Mae between holding hands with both of them.

As they rounded the covered wagon, fixed up inside as living quarters, a boy of about six stuck his head out to whine, "I can't sleep, Mom. I feel like I'm being punished when you send me to bed without supper and I ain't *done* nothing, durn it!"

His young mother replied, "Just lie still and count backwards from a hundred like I told you, Raymond."

Longarm said, "I got a better idea, Miss Nell. Why don't I run back to our wagon for, say, a sack of flour, a side of bacon and some canned peaches we brung along?"

"Only on condition that you let us write you an I.O.U. . . . Canada," she said. "My husband will want to repay you in cash as soon as he comes back from Leadville. You see, he had to go up to Leadville to arrange another loan and . . . he ought to be back any time now."

Longarm turned to head back to his own claim without comment. If she thought you rode to another mining district to interest investors in a try hole he had no call to dispute the word of a man he'd never met.

As long as he was about it, knowing how long cooking seemed to take when you were a hungry kid, Longarm gathered up some canned beans and tomato preserves, putting them in an empty burlap bag with the flour, bacon and canned fruit.

Once he had them up to the Fordham claim, nobody had much to say as Nell Fordham sobbed, "Oh, Sweet Mary, Mother of God, bless you!" and fell on the fresh supplies like a mother wolf with cubs to feed.

He'd been right to fetch grub you didn't need to cook. He felt obliged to warn her not to overfeed her hungry kids and she remembered civilized eating habits in time to keep from harming them. But they both fell asleep sitting up without finishing their peaches. As he helped her put the two of them to bed in the wagon, Nell confided, "They were exhausted but too hungry to fall asleep, earlier."

Then she covered her face with her hands and sobbed, "Whatever must you think of me? A woman scorned who can't feed her own children. You will be gentle, won't you? I haven't . . . been with a man for some time, but I'll do my best by you, whenever you're ready."

Longarm hadn't eaten any of the grub he'd brought and

her coffee had been just awful. Blowing a smoke ring from the cheroot he'd been working on as he sat across the fire from her, Longarm said, "I thought we had agreed the grub was just a loan 'til your man got back from Leadville, Miss Nell."

She stared bitterly into the glowing coals between them as she answered, "We both know better than that, don't we? We were up here trying to save our marriage for the sake of the children. He'd lost his job in Kansas, as he was losing me, to a drinking problem. He swore he'd be able to stay sober, up here in the mountains with something to keep him busy as he worked to make us rich. Maybe it would have worked, had he found any color before the last of our money ran out. If the truth be known, it was my money, an inherited nest egg from another foolish woman inclined to trust sweet-talking drunkards but who nonetheless wound up with her own parlor house."

Longarm had heard the same story before. But it was more polite to hear a wronged woman out than to ask her to shut the hell up.

He sat there as the coals grew ever dimmer, smoking more than one cheroot in silence as he heard how most every man on earth but him had taken cruel advantage of the poor trusting gal. Albeit, when you went over it some, it developed she'd only been married twice before. She'd simply made it *sound* like a regiment lined up to use and abuse her.

There came a lull in the conversation. Then she suddenly blurted, "I understand those wicked women at the Crystal Palace make as much in a night as a hard-rock miner takes home in a week! Could that be true?"

Longarm said, "A working gal can make more than *that* if she really puts her *back* into it. But you don't want to take up that line of work, Miss Nell, and I was just about to tell you the sad story of another respectable lady who thought she'd been betrayed by her man out this way."

He let that sink in and continued, "They were newly wedded and out to get rich quick in the high country when, like your man, he allowed he had to tend beeswax in other parts, leaving his little woman alone with the bills piling up, as they tend to, sudden, in mining country."

She said, "I know the feeling! Do you know they ask as much as a dollar for one fresh egg in town?"

Longarm said, "It's a seller's market. Worse than being aboard a cross-country train at the mercy of the candy snatcher. So, anyhow, this mining man seemed to vanish into thin air and after his woman had waited a spell, she heard talk about him and a painted lady of the town who seemed to be missing as well."

He blew another smoke ring, barely visible above the remains of the fire, and said, "Great minds must run in the same . . . dirty channels. This other gal we're talking about decided she could be a painted lady, too, if that was what men wanted. So she went bad. Really bad. Wound up the most bawdy painted dove in Colorado for a spell. We don't know one another well enough for me to describe what she'd do three ways for two dollars."

Nell said, "Oh, you can tell me, seeing we're friends talking in the dark like. . . . Pray continue."

Longarm said, "One day a lawman came to the house of ill repute she now frequented. He had with him a pocket Bible. In it there was a loving inscription signed by her in her own hand. She recognized it as a wedding gift she'd picked out for her man, before he'd done her dirty with that other wicked woman."

"How did the law come by such a thing?" asked Nell.

Longarm said, "They'd just found it in the bottom of an abandoned mine shaft, along with what remained of her missing husband. You see, he'd never run off on her in the first place. He'd fallen down or been thrown down that abandoned mine shaft to just lie there, all that time his woman was making a name for herself as the lowest slut west of the Big Muddy."

Nell sighed and said, "I'm sure she felt awful and it was a nice try. But I know the man I married and he hasn't fallen down any mine shaft. He's simply abandoned us as a burden that interferes with his drinking!"

Longarm grunted to his feet, saying, "Let's give him to the end of the week. If you still want to become a whore, I'll be proud to let you suck my cock before I ram it up your ass."

She gasped, "Oh, my God, is that any way to speak to a woman?"

He asked in a deliberately brutal tone, "How do you expect a horny hard-rock miner with a silver dollar in one fist and his cock in the other to put it? You were the one, just now, so intent on becoming a whore. It ain't a delicate profession, Miss Nell. Wait 'til you get to service a gang of really nasty drunks!"

She gasped, "Maybe we'd better give my man to the end of the week, and perhaps I ought to thank you for striking a light to my self-pitying daydreams. I know I'd never be able to live that life. Just thinking about . . . you know, with you alone, made me go all funny inside."

He didn't answer. She explained, "You see, sitting here alone with two hungry children had me thinking up all sorts of ways for us to manage our way back to Kansas. But when you came along, as flesh and blood instead of a fantasy . . ."

He cut in, "I figured as much, Miss Nell. I'll be going back to my own tent, now. The grub I . . . loaned you ought to last you through a day or more. We'll talk about getting you all back to Kansas later in the week, after we've both had time to do some calculations."

She rose in the dark but he left without waiting to see if she wanted to swap spit or just shake. He knew human nature, including his own, too well to move farther down that slippery slope.

Back in the tent, shucking most of his duds to turn in, Longarm had a hunch he knew how this was likely to turn out and he sensed he'd never forgive himself, either way.

He was almost there but still awake when old Buck floundered in, half drunk but sensible enough, for himself, to declare, "Don't never play cards with that one tinhorn they call Major Manson. After I'd paid for a little consolation, I was busted. You're going to have to advance me more pocket jingle, pard."

Longarm started to argue, snorted in disgust and decided, "We can talk about it tomorrow afternoon. Late in the afternoon. We got us a long day ahead of us, Buck."

"How come? What are we going to do?" the beefy Texican asked.

Longarm said, "Along about noon we'll blast that face we spent the morning drilling and charging, as far as anyone else can tell. Before you get all hystericated, I've set the charge under loose muck we won't have to bring down the hard way. After we give everyone around us a good thump to recall, if asked, we'll haul some shattered granite out to dump as our tailings from all that earlier effort. Then, as you hold the fort, I'll take samples into town to be assayed."

Skane sat on his own bunk in the dark, muttering, "I don't get it. What's the sense of asking them to assay ore you know to be worthless? Won't they tell you there's no gold in it?"

Longarm replied, "I just said that. It would look suspicious as hell if we struck pay dirt a blast or so after those others gave up. I figure we ought to work this claim to around the end of the week before we take in some color."

The big towhead flopped flat with his boots on as he muttered in a tone of likkered-up disgust, "That's when you'll strike color by magic, right? I hope I can keep from having to gun that surly stringbean down to the next claim before we're rich."

"Mr. Growly Bear?" asked Longarm in sudden interest, adding, "I understand he bites the toes off little girls. What did he say he meant to bite off you, Buck?"

The Texican said, "Nothing. He called me a son of a bitch and I told him to take that back or fill his fist. So he did and I warned him the eyes of Texas were upon him."

"How come all this happened?" Longarm asked.

Skane said, "Beat the shit out of me. I was walking out here by starlight when this cuss yelled out from the dark that I was a son of bitch trespassing on his claim. I left him with the understanding he'd wind up buried on his claim if he ever called this child a son of a bitch again. If there's one thing I can't abide, it's surly neighbors."

Longarm smiled up in the dark as he agreed, "I know what you mean. But at least the folk up the *other* way seem friendly enough."

Chapter 8

They spent most of the next day going through the motions and making the noises anyone watching would expect. Knowing it took most of a shift for an experienced crew to drill and set charges, Longarm killed some of the time on a worthwhile project, feeling dumb for not having thought of it until Willie Mae Fordham had jogged his memory the night before.

It killed the better part of an hour to dig a simple square pit for the dynamite left, which was, of course, most of it. He meant to save the sticks he'd salted with gold leaf for last. But they remained perforce in the one box he'd opened.

As long as they had time to spare, and to refresh his own mind as well as his hands, Longarm showed Buck how to drill granite the hard way.

It was easy to see why the new "steam drills," actually run by air compressed by a moveable steam engine, had proven so wildly popular. The Burleigh drill made deep mining and projects like the famous Sutro tunnel of Nevada possible.

Up until its introduction in the early 1870s, along with the prefabricated Deidesheimer timber frame, aurifeous rock had been drilled one sledgehammer blow at a time with the star drill, a length of octagonal steel filed to a multiple chisel point.

One man held the drill bit in place, trustingly, while the other struck repeated blows with his nine-pound sledge, with each blow dislodging a few grains of rock. His partner gave the bit a quarter turn with every blow. It seemed to take forever to get a drill hole started but in fact the bit sank faster once the hole was a few inches deep and lubricated with water to hold some of the grit and help the steel cut.

They actually managed a couple of yard-deep holes in the time two Cousin Jacks might have drilled the whole face. Longarm let them be but explained to his bemused sidekick how the capped and fused stick of dynamite went in, the charge was tamped with clay and everybody got the hell out of there as first some slow and then the quick fuse burned down to set off the charges.

Skane scuffed the already blasted free rock along the base of the face with his steel-toed boot as he said, "So this is what you wind up with and then what?"

Longarm said, "Watch where you plant your feet. There's capped and fused dynamite under that muck. They call it muck because the next thing you do is muck it into that wheelbarrow, or a tram car if we get serious, and haul it out to that long pile of tailings, topside. Then we have a sample of the fresh ore run and if there's color after all, we dray the muck over to the crushers and let them handle it from there on. There's more than one way to reduce a given ore and hundreds of ways the color you want can mix with minerals you don't."

Lighting a smoke but shaking his head when Skane made as if to head up the slope for some fresh air, Longarm continued, "When the metal's formed a chemical combination with unwanted chlorine, sulfur and such, extraction gets tricky. Since we're about to strike a barely paying amalgam of native or pure metallic gold and granite, most of the gold would be in or along the edges of those quartz veins, so they'll probably suggest mercury reduction. It's more expensive but quicker and more thorough than running crushed rock slurry over riffles. Gold melts into mercury like sugar melts into water. So you mix the rock flour in mercury a spell and as the feldspar mica, silica and such works its way to the surface of the heavier mercury, it leaves all its golden atoms behind."

"Can we go topside and eat now?" asked Buchanan T.

Longarm said, "We ain't done charging all the holes we drilled yet. So pay attention. Mining men are supposed to know some of this shit."

Old Buck sat down on the empty wheelbarrow. Longarm said, "Once all the crushed rock separates from the mercury, they brush it off and pour the mercury into a sort of whiskey still. You don't want your mercury boiling away in thin air as you heat it up. It's expensive to begin with and pure poison if you breath the fumes."

"Why boil it in the first place, then?" asked his far from eager pupil.

Longarm said, "Much the same reasons you boil a mix of alcohol and water. To separate 'em. Mercury is molten metal at room temperature and boils to a vapor on a kitchen stove. The gold dissolved in it, having the boiling point of a noble metal, stays put and you wind up with a pot of gold and a pot of recovered mercury, see?"

The beefy Texican said, "If you say so. Let's go eat. It's way after noon, damn it!"

Longarm consulted his watch, shrugged and bent over to light an exposed length of slow fuse as he calmly declared, "Fire in the hole. Let's go eat."

They'd made it around the tent to commence opening cans when the ground beneath them shuddered and the adit across their claim cleared its throat with a deep rumble and coughed a cloud of dust.

Up to the north the Fordham kids ran around their

wagon to stare and wave. Longarm waved back. Goldberg to the south, along with his helper, who looked to be a breed or Mex kid, popped out for a look-see. When Longarm waved Goldberg never waved back.

"Fuck you." Longarm smiled, breaking out some pork and beans.

Skane said, "Gents go crazy, away from the soothing influence of womankind. Takes occasional conversation with a woman to keep a man's head on his shoulders. When Greek Gloria told me I was babbling like a brook in bed I saw I'd been spending too much time alone in my blanket roll of late. A man's mind wanders all over creation as he stares up at the stars, wondering how high the sky goes."

Longarm said, "Ain't got time to brew coffee if we mean to muck that ore and let me run a sample into town. Tomato preserves cut the greasy aftertaste of the pork almost as good as coffee."

Old Buck was saying, "I mean it stands to reason the sky can't go up and up and up without never ending. But if you imagine a big black ceiling way up yonder, you're stuck with the up and up on the *far side* of the same. How come you put all that dirt back in the hole if you only meant to muck it out, and what do we do with it after that?"

Longarm said, "Late tonight, with nobody looking, we wheelbarrow a few tons back down so's we can muck it tomorrow, unless you'd care to drill that whole fucking face and do her for real."

Skane grunted, "That'll be the day. You remind me of the way gals put me back on the tracks. I don't mean I'm queer for you or nothing. But I have noticed, and been grateful, how a gal can stop a man's mind from thinking in circles."

He chuckled and added, "I'm reminded of this gal in San Antone, one time. A Mex gal, had a cross over her bed, and you hear how religious they can get. But as I got to wondering who created God if God created everything else, she said, *"¿Quien sabe?"* and then got on top and I forgot all about God for a spell. Later, when I asked her if she ever worried about such shit, she said she found God's creations confusing enough without worrying about their creator. How come I can't be like that, pard? How come I get to wondering how long forever will last and why some of us are born rich and others so poor. I've never enjoyed being poor and it hardly seems fair."

Longarm shrugged and said, "Things could have been worse. You could have been born a Mex gal with some ass-hole asking her who created God. Or for that matter you could have been created a mayfly and grown old and died without ever *getting* to wonder about what the fuck was going on."

"What the fuck *is* going on?" asked Buchanan T. a spell later as they dumped the last of that day's "production" on the long-rambling windrow of tailings along the south boundry of their claim.

Longarm said, "I told you. I take a sample in to Pot Luck and pay to have it assayed."

"But you know it's worthless rock!" pouted old Buck, adding, "And that reminds me. I'm tapped out. I need at least some tobacco money, damn it!"

Longarm reached into his dusty jeans to fish out a cart-wheel, saying as he handed it over, "Here, in case some-body comes by selling door-to-door. We'll talk about your allowance after I get back. You're starting to be an expensive little darling to spoon with and I have to see about getting us more money. It's easy to see Billy Vail might not have allocated half enough."

Longarm took off his sweaty shirt and treated himself to a whore bath with canteen water. It was easier, now, to see why so many mining men grew beards. His stubble just looked untidy, so far.

He donned a fresh shirt, strapped on his gun rig and

perched his peaked cap at a jauntier angle than he usually wore his pancaked Stetson. Then he picked up the ore samples he'd loaded into that same burlap bag, told his sidekick he might be late and headed into Pot Luck.

First things coming first, he trudged south into the complex of stamping mills, smelters and such that made Pot Luck seem, to its south, a sort of little Pittsburgh, albeit the famous Leadville mine of that name had been named by a prospector called Hook who'd worked in a steel mill in the bigger Pittsburgh before Silver Dollar Tabor wound up owning it.

Few if any mines seemed to remain in the hands of the prospectors who'd located them. It took one sort of mind to search for treasures in the raw and another kind entire to shuffle wealth on paper.

At the dinky assay office, located betwixt a coal tipple and a saloon, Longarm was told, firmly but not unkindly, he'd brought them no more than busted-up granite laced with pure quartz. When Longarm hopefully remarked on a metallic golden tinge to some of the nodules of quartz, the old assay man shook his head like a kindly grandfather explaining bumps in the night to a kid and said, "Iron pyrites, fool's gold, and just a trace of the same. Must have been some sulfuric acid in the vein before it filled with quartz. Iron turns that golden shade, mixed with sulfur. If the crystals were bigger you could see they're cubic, which gold is not."

Longarm had known that. The other glitter in granite that wasn't gold was mica. He paid for the assay like a sport and the assayer said he'd get rid of his worthless rock for him. So he headed next for a Western Union closer to the narrow-guage tracks.

As he was going in, a handsome but worried-looking gal was coming out. She dismissed him with a glance. That was what happened when a man wore faded denim and didn't shave regular. Her tan, poplin travel duster was earning its keep amid the gritty confusion of Pot Luck, and her pretty face, despite the veiled riding derby, was about due for washing, if not a shave. After that, she had dusty dark hair and her rear view wasn't bad, either, as Longarm turned to admire her walking on up the way.

It didn't hurt a gal to be admired, as long as nobody whistled.

As Billy Vail had long since explained to all his deputies, you could try to send secret messages in code or cipher. Billy Vail forbade his deputies to wire ciphered messages, with each letter replaced by another, because anybody who knew how they worked would spot one at a glance and it would take only an hour or less to decipher it.

Coded messages were meant to look like something else in plain English. So they might not attract anyone's eyes to begin with, and after that the reader had to know what the sender and receiver had agreed upon in advance.

Wiring home about feeling optimistic or not could mean anything to the pals reading it. Longarm truthfully told his Aunt Tilly at another deputy's home address that he'd bought into a claim and hadn't struck color, so far. Then he said he was a tad worried about one of his mules not being willing to pull its weight and showing signs of hoof and mouth disease. He left it to his elders to agree or disagree it was time to consider new livestock, and a mining man who whined prices in a mining camp were dearer than expected was by definition a mining man who'd spent little time in mining camps.

Then seeing it was going on sunset and there'd been no caffeine in those tomato preserves out to the claim, Longarm repaired to the hotel they'd stayed at to see if he might order a meal in their dining room.

In the lobby they said he could and he ducked in across the way to allow he'd like black coffee with his steak smothered in the tasty little wild onions growing up their way.

As he waited, that same handsome brunetter he'd seen

by the telegraph office came in, having shed her duster and veiled hat and looking way neater with her face washed and hair freshly brushed. Her summer dress was beige pongee. She filled the tailored bodice just right and to his pleasant surprise, came over to his table to smile down at him uncertain and exclaim, "*Pardonnez-moi, M'sieur, mais parlez-vous Quebecais?*"

To which Longarm could only reply, rising to his feet and doffing his miner's cap, "I know just enough French Canadian to allow I don't speak much, ma'am."

She was flustered. "Oh, they told me in the lobby you were called Canada and I thought . . ."

Longarm knew better than to bluff what seemed the real thing. So he said, "Some call me that because I panned for color up in your Peace River country one time, ma'am. Had I found any I might still be there. But I never did. So here I am in Colorado. How may I serve you?"

When she asked if she might join him for a moment, Longarm moved around to help her with her chair and ask what she'd be having. She allowed she wasn't up to more than coffee. As the two of them settled in, she told him her own name was Theresa Ferrier but her friends all called her Risa. She was in Pot Luck looking for her brother, Jacques, who hadn't wired or written since he'd bragged on hitting it rich six weeks earlier.

Risa said, "He stayed in this hotel while he worked his claim somewhere out there. I haven't been able to determine where. When I heard you were called Canada, and that you'd recently stayed here . . ."

Longarm cut in to say, "Lord love you, it won't work, Miss Risa. Me and my sidekick, who's from Texas, just got here. If your brother ain't been seen here at this hotel for six weeks, he was long gone before we got here. But what might he look like and how come you can't locate his claim?"

She described her brother as four years older than she

with a family resemblance and a game leg he favored with a cane. Then she asked why Longarm had seemed so puzzled about her not knowing where her missing brother had been moiling for gold. She said nobody she'd asked had been able to tell her.

He said, "If your brother filed a mining claim, it would still be on file, Miss Risa. Mining claims are filed with the Federal Bureau of Mines with one copy going to Washington. Didn't nobody tell you that?"

She said nobody had, and she'd asked a lot of men in a lot of places.

The waitress brought his order and he told her the lady would be having coffee. As the waitress left for the kitchen to fetch some, the Canadian gal looked as if she was about to blubber up. So he said, "Don't take it personal, ma'am. Heaps of men from other parts go missing up here in the high country and why they might have done so is considered their own beeswax. Gents out our way get reluctant to gossip about others they may or may not have seen in passing. Sometimes gents who wanted to stay lost come after a gossip with a gun."

"But you seem willing to help me," she demured.

Longarm said, "Your story makes sense to me. Or mayhaps I have hidden reasons to worry about missing French Canadians. His being a subject of Her Majesty, Victoria, would mean more papers than usual to file. Since I've filed more mining claims than I like to think of in my day, I know who to wire in Washington. It may take us a day or more for them to get around to wiring back, though."

She clapped her hands and said, "Oh, bless you! I don't want to hurry your meal, but . . ."

He chuckled and said, "Western Union's open all night, which is more than can be said for the Bureau of Mines in Washington, ma'am. Why don't we settle your flutters with some pie à la mode along with your coffee before we amble back to that telegraph office?"

He cut into his steak as he quietly added, "We got all night to work with. So why don't we just sort of ease into the same?"

Chapter 9

Longarm spent most of his suppertime undressing Risa
Ferrier with his eyes. He hadn't been getting any lately but
he had to consider how he was going to build a fire under
the file clerks in Washington. He knew your average citizen
signing his inquiry "Cooper" would be lucky to get an answer in eight weeks. Western Union clerks got fired for re-
vealing private messages to others. But U.S. senators had
been known to take bribes and something funny was going
on in Pot Luck. So he decided to send one wire as Cooper
and follow it up with a later wire to his Aunt Tilly so's
Henry could let the Bureau of Mines know on the sly it was
a federal inquiry.

He suspected she might not have been getting any lately
either when, before he'd finished his peach cobbler dessert,
she asked why a man his age was out to grow a beard. She
asked 'in that light tone women reserve for gentle nagging
before they feel they have the Indian sign on a man.

When Longarm explained about razor scrapes and the
fetid air underground, she allowed she understood and
should have thought of that. Then she said he'd still look
nicer if he shaved more often.

He said he meant to treat himself to a sit-down shave

and a manicure as soon as he and his Texas pard struck color. He explained, "Plutocrats like Silver Dollar Tabor and Leadville Johnny Brown don't have to go down in their mines. Once they commence to turn some profit, these hills are full of men willing to work a mine for three dollars a shift."

She said she'd read in the papers about threats of a general strike.

He shrugged and said, "I'll pay three-fifty and still let a barber muck my chin whilst a pretty little thing soaks my fingers in rose water. Nobody would crawl around under these mountains for one day if he wasn't hoping to wind up high on the hog."

She sighed and said, "You sound just like my brother Jacques. We had a modestly profitable family business in Montreal when he read about so many Canadians making names for themselves out here in your West."

Longarm washed down some dessert and soberly replied, "The two Canucks who come first to mind, no offense, would be Sandy McSween down Lincoln County way and Bat Masterson, whose Canadian brother got shot in Dodge a spell back. Bat's still with us, but McSween's pushing up clover, too. It seems easier for a body to make a name for himself out here dead than alive, and you say old Jacques had a thriving business back home?"

He saw he'd said too much when she dabbed her eyes and sobbed, "I *told* him not to run off like Don Quixote, and we haven't heard a word about or from him for over a month!"

Longarm left most of his dessert on the plate to drain his cup and suggest they go send some wires.

They did and doing so seemed to cheer her some. They walked back to the same hotel arm in arm. By the time they arrived, Longarm had a hard-on. He suspected from her flushed cheeks as they entered the lamplit lobby the feeling might be mutual. But Longarm had long since learned the hard way to let the lady decide when she was ready for you to reel her in.

Many a man, including his younger self, had blown a sure thing with an awkward early move. So when she smiled up at him by lamplight to ask him when he might be back with word from Washington, Longarm said he had to do some drilling and blasting the next day but suggested they might sup together whether any word had come by wire or not. He explained he meant to ask around town about young Canadians who looked sort of French, no offense, and walked with a cane.

Then he quit whilst he was ahead, even though he'd wanted to kiss her so bad he could taste it.

His erection had subsided by the time he made it over to the Crystal Palace. As he'd hoped, the night was still young but a couple of games were in progress. Longarm ordered a beer and a fresh deck of cards at the bar, with his back to the crowd and nobody in it having any reason to pay any mind to a sort of shabby cuss dressed more for mining than other games of chance.

Pocketing the cards and nursing the lager, Longarm strolled over to sip silently, leaning against the back wall, as he watched one game from a polite distance.

It took him the first beer, sipped slow, to determine that the professional in the game, a benign-looking white-haired gent they called Major Manson, was a mechanic. Wandering off and returning later with another beer, Longarm didn't take too much longer to make certain the smiling old fart with eyes of cold steel was a *cautious* mechanic who only won more often than he lost and, better yet, knew better than to deal himself anything more suspicious than four of a kind after dealing his marks, say, flushes or full houses.

Four of a kind was only the third-best hand possible in a poker game. But four cards of the same denomination, along with the fifth left over, beat the three-to-two ration of a full house or the five cards of any single suit you called a flush.

Since the odds of an honest deal awarding you a flush or full house were astronomical, the mark who found his fool self holding either was inclined to raise more than once before you showed him an only slightly better hand and, when you did, he was likely to be a sport about it as long as you didn't overdo it.

Gents who suspected dirty dealing expected to see a royal flush, or a ten, jack, king and queen with an ace. So Longarm figured on winning just one good pot with the straight flush the major seemed too modest to deal himself.

To do so, he bode his time and sat down casually after an older man declared he'd lost enough for one night and got up from the table. Longarm had already gotten rid of his own deck of cards in the crap house. When you didn't need 'em, extra cards could be embarrassing, and the major's smooth methods made him a lamb ripe for the shearing.

Since nobody halfway honest was expected to start winning from the get-go, and since Longarm's even slicker method took some time, he played an honest but conservative game, passing when he drew a modest hand and betting sensibly when the major delt him higher hopes. There were now six men at the table. So the major only got to deal every sixth hand and that kept things going smoothly for him. He played honestly when it hadn't been his deal and a man could keep from losing big if he didn't bluff or raise too recklessly.

As the game progressed, Longarm was naturally dealt all sorts of cards. It was easy enough to hang on to the few he wanted and casually discard the rest. He only needed to hold out five from a deck of fifty-two and it wasn't easy to keep count of had anyone been trying.

When he had his straight flush of three, four, five, six and seven of hearts in his lap, Longarm switched them with the tempting but not good enough full house the major had dealt him before he suddenly seemed to take more interest in the game.

Everyone but the major dropped out, one by one, as the two of them kept raising the table stakes as if they surely had something going for them. The major, knowing he'd dealt himself the winning hand, was smart enough to call as others drifted over to see what all the excitement was about. The major was content with less than a thousand in the pot.

Or he would have been, had not the unkempt "Canada" spread a straight flush instead of the full house he'd been dealt on the table to calmly rake in his winnings.

"Hold on!" the major declared abruptly, his eyes staring as warmly as those of a king cobra made of spring steel, "Those are not the cards . . . I expected you to have."

Longarm managed to spill some cards on the floor as he was pocketing his winnings, allowing him to put all the cards back as he replied in a jovial tone, "Of course you thought I was holding another hand, Major. You'd have been an idjet to raise against a straight flush with no better than four of a kind."

The major decided, "You're likely right. Why don't we settle by just cutting the cards, winner take all?"

By way of emphasis he placed a pearly handled Colt Lighting on the table between them. Somebody muttered, "Jesus!" and the two of them now had that corner table all to themselves.

Longarm rose to his considerable height, his Schofield remaining handy enough in its cross-draw holster as he smiled down to reply, "I reckon I've wagered as much as I care to this evening, Major. I got to get back out to my claim if it's all the same with you."

The older man got to his own feet, putting the double-action six-gun on the table as he purred, "It's not all the same with me, pilgrim. I just offered to cut the cards like a sport. Are you the sort who quits whilst he's ahead without giving his friends a sporting chance?"

Longarm said, "I sure am. That's the only way you ever come out ahead at anything in life. By quitting whilst you're ahead."

He let that sink in before he added, "I saw a situation like this up in the Montana gold fields one time. Poor loser decided to shoot it out with a stranger he'd never met up with before. He should have quit whilst he was ahead."

The major tried, "I'm a stranger to you as well, am I not?"

Longarm stared him right in the eye as he replied, "I've met you, or gents just like you, before."

Then he turned his back on the tinhorn and walked out with his winnings, knowing how often a professional shot a man in the back in front of a saloon full of witnesses. But some in the crowd seemed impressed as hell. Somebody whispered, "Who in thunder *is* that tall drink of water?"

As he was leaving, another member of the crowd declaimed, "They call him Canada. Whoever he is, he just backed Major Manson down and they say the major's nobody to mess with!"

Time seemed to fly when you were having fun. So Longarm found himself on the dark, nigh-empty main street of Pot Luck after midnight with more money than he'd started out with.

Seizing opportunity by the forelock, having the night and Western Union alone, he went back to the telegraph office to compose and send a night letter to his Aunt Tilly, advising her he'd sent that wire about that earlier claim to the Bureau of Mines.

As soon as he read the night letter, Old Billy Vail, if not Henry, would know enough to wire the Bureau of Mines about any messages from Miner Cooper and once the Bureau of Mines knew they were supposed to—damn it—answer, they'd need no further directions.

He paid for the wire himself, knowing a real prospector would hardly charge one to the Justice Department, and as long as he was about it, had them change some of the major's specie into paper money he could tuck away in his gun belt.

On a hunch he circled wide, going uphill through the shanty town of frame and canvas, in case the major or anyone else might be interested in all that ready cash.

He moved upslope well north of the tent where old Buck was minding the store if he had a lick of sense and dropped over the granite reef north of the Fordham claim. As he moved south along the footpatch, he saw Nell's night fire had gone out. She was likely asleep in the wagon with her kids. But he had to do what he had to do. So he softly hailed the camp as he got closer.

Nell Fordham wasn't in her wagon. She'd been sitting alone in the dark by the adit of her missing man's try hole. Too worried, she said, to turn in.

There was no moon and bright as the stars were at that altitude he could only make out her outline as he hunkered down beside her with his back braced against the outcrop. She seemed to be sitting on a box or a bucket. He said, "I'm riding a lucky streak this evening, Miss Nell, and feeling lucky. So what if you sold me your unproven claim, as is, for, say, five hundred dollars?"

She gasped, "Are you serious? I tried to borrow a hundred dollars worth of credit on this hole in the ground and they told me there were lots of holes in the ground up this way."

She sighed and added, "They told me surveyors who know about such things doubt the ever-narrowing lode of lead-silver chloride under some claims to the south extend this far north."

Longarm said, "Me and old Buck ain't after lead or silver, and gold is where you find it, Miss Nell. If there's any in the rock we've been working, some of it might extend on up the reef. If there ain't no gold, there ain't no gold and we're not going to die rich after all."

He let that sink in before he said, "That's life. We take our chances. Let me buy you out for more than enough to see you and your kids back to Kansas and I'll tell you what, I'll leave you a ten percent share on paper in case we all get lucky."

She didn't answer for a long time. It sounded as if she was trying not to blubber up. When she did speak, she said, "You're trying to spare our pride, aren't you? We both know there's no color here. The father of those children left us broke and hungry by a worthless claim and . . . Oh, Canada, I don't know what to say!"

He murmured, "Say yes and rustle up your papers so's I can buy them off you before you change your mind. I can have the lawyer who did the paperwork on our other claim transfer yours to me and old Buck if you trust me for my I.O.U. on that ten percent share."

She sobbed, "You know I have to say yes, you gallant fool! But . . . why, if you don't want to . . . you know?"

He said, "Oh, I *want* to, being a natural man, and I'd like to think we'd both enjoy it. But us Don Quixotes are funny that way. One of these days I may start shaving again and, when I do, I want to be able to meet my own eye without blinking."

She murmured, "I know what you mean. But be it known you *could* have. A woman with hungry children to feed can't afford to feel proud."

Then she sobbed, "Oh, Canada, how *else* can I thank you for letting me go on feeling proud?"

He said, "By feeling proud, of course. Let's get them papers before I change my mind and we both wind up feeling low by the cold gray dawn!"

So that was what they did and Longarm continued on to his own camp with a raging hard-on and less some poker winnings. It hardly seemed fair Willie Mae would grow up hearing how some fool called Canada had been such a fuckless saint. But on reflection, a man who wanted to be recalled as a saint under his right name was a sort of four-flusher. So what the hell.

Moving quietly into their tent so as not to disturb old Buck, Longarm found the towhead awake.

As Longarm sat down to shuck his clothes, the sidekick imposed on him said he'd been up past midnight, bullshitting with old Goldberg from the claim to their south.

The Texican said, "He ain't such a bad old bird when you get to know him. He came up this evening to allow he was sorry for cussing me out the other night. Brung a jug of white lightning as a peace offering. So now we're at peace with the old Jew bastard. Ain't that a bitch?"

Longarm said, "Better peace than war," as he unbuckled his gun belt and got to work on his buttons.

Buchanan T. woke him up again by smugly saying, "I made us a tidy little profit on what was left of that open box of dynamite."

"You *what?*" blinked Longarm.

The pain in the ass he'd only wanted to get shed of, up until then, calmly told him, "Old Goldberg said he was low on dynamite. Wanted to know if we had any to spare, saving him a trudge into town in the morning. I sold him the loose sticks we had left, making a dime profit on each and every stick. Ain't that a bitch?"

Chapter 10

The fat was in the fire. Kicking the shit out Buchanan T. would have felt good but it wouldn't have gotten the fat out of the fire. At least the asshole's blunder helped Longarm to refrain from thinking about a willing woman just up the damned reef—if only he hadn't been raised by a mother who, homespun or not, had been a lady.

Even though he'd turned in well after midnight, he had one long night of tossing and turning as he considered all the ways things might turn out. He kept warning himself that anything he did now was likely to make things even worse.

Old Goldberg wouldn't get his day's worth of muck assayed until later the coming afternoon and, what the hell, the poor old cuss had been *drilling* for *color*. If he drilled deeper on false hopes, he'd no doubt stop before he got to China or, what the hell, drill on down to the real things. You just never knew up this way.

He was too tuckered and Skane hadn't wheeled any tailing back down to the face, as he'd been asked. Longarm muttered, "Fuck it. I got chores in town in any case."

Next morning, fixing breakfast, Longarm saw no signs of movement down at Goldberg's claim. The loner was likely already down in his try hole, in for a pleasant surprise before sundown.

He saw no action up at the Fordham claim as he and old Buck got going. Around nine, Longarm moseyed on up, warning the tingle in his jeans not to get an idea, dammit.

When he got there he found the covered wagon with most of it's rumpled bedding and a rag doll little Willie Mae had left behind. Nell and her kids had left on foot, well before cock's-crow, with what little they really needed as they legged it south to the narrow-guage and Kansas.

Standing there alone, Longarm lit a cheroot as he said aloud with a knowing smile, "Great minds run in the same channels and folk who know their own weaknesses quit whilst they're ahead. So *via con Dios*, Miss Nell, and I reckon we were right."

Walking slowly back to his own camp in the crisp morning light as a mocking bird called him a fool, Longarm found himself humming an old song he hadn't studied on for a spell. It went . . .

> "Nelly was a lady,
> Last night she died.
> Toll the bell for lovely Nell,
> My lost Virginee bride."

Then he laughed and said, "Bride my ass. We never even kissed." But he still had a time getting the tune out of his head all morning.

Feeling no call to mess with those safely stabled mules for such light hauling, Longarm took their wheelbarrow in with him, walking ahead of it with the handles forward. When he got to Zip Finny's general store, he asked if he might leave it there a spell, explaining he meant to wheel more dynamite out to the claim.

Zip Finny said, "You boys drilled in that much already? You must both be part beaver."

"Paid some old boys down on their luck to spell us on the star drill," Longarm lied, fishing out Nell's papers as he added, "Just bought us the Fordham claim up the line. Owner had to leave sudden for Kansas and we didn't have much time for . . . fussing with papers. Could you have the same lawyer tidy these up so's they read right, with me and old Buck holding both claims?"

Finny said, "Sure. But it's going to cost you another filing fee and lawyers have to eat, too. How come you bought that unproven Fordham claim, Canada? They tell me at the assay office nobody's been working her for a spell."

Longarm nodded easily and said, "That's why me and old Buck aim to work her, some. Can we settle up when I come back for that dynamite?"

Zip Finny said they sure could and Longarm left. As he vanished up Main Street, another customer who'd been examining the hell out of some hardware a few yards off sidled closer to state firmly, "They're *on* to something. When a man with a claim commences to spend freely without that hungry look to him, he's on to something. Who is he, Zip?"

Finny said, "They call him Canada. He seems like a friendly enough cuss but they say it's best not to mess with him. Packs the same hardware as Cole Younger and they say he crawfished Major Manson just last night."

"Manson ain't no mining man," said the mining man who'd been listening.

Zip Finny replied, "I know. The major's a hard case most men out our way are scared to cross. They say old Canada told him to go fuck hisself and then turned his back on him as if to dare him to try!"

The other local whistled and decided, "Forget I asked. As far as this child cares, old Canada can buy out all the claims he wants."

Then he added with a wink, "I still say he's *on* to something!"

What Longarm was on to was a noon dinner, hoping he might have company.

He didn't call at the hotel desk for Risa Ferrier. He didn't have a good excuse to, yet, and next to walking a picket fence for a gal there was nothing more likely to cross her legs than calling on her with no excuse.

Had some nosy guardian angel asked, Longarm would have pointed out that a desperate young mother with hungry kids on her empty hands was one thing and a gal who spoke French and owned her own business was another.

The sticking point, had Longarm thought about it, was the notion of a man paying cold hard cash. Men always paid. That was a given. What Professor Darwin called natural evolution had long since separated women from lost causes who expected nothing. The human species was mostly descended from men who'd treated women decent and women who'd expected to be treated decent. So it was natural for any gal to expect at least flowers, books and candy from a swain. Longarm just felt awkward paying cash on the barrelhead. He felt better spending a hundred dollars to show a gal a good time than asking her what she'd do for a dollar down and the rest when through, like that song they sang about the ring dang doo.

When he thought about it, he had to admit his delicate feeling made no sense. But when you *thought* about it, the sensible course was to keep your fool pecker in your pants and say no more about it. Professor Darwin had warned neither salmon, bees nor humankind were allowed to show such good sense if they expected to evolve.

Risa Ferrier never came into her hotel dining room for dinner, not knowing he was there, so after he'd dawdled there through three cups of coffee he wheeled the extra dynamite back to their claim and warned old Buck to never—dammit—do that again.

Skane wanted to go into Pot Luck and get laid with his profits from the night before. Longarm said, "Go ahead.

Kiss her once for me. But get back before sundown. I got other fish to fry in town tonight."

Skane said, "That hardly sounds fair. I was stuck out here last night."

Longarm said, "I was making money hand over fist, and you just said you aimed to get laid this afternoon. They never sent us up this way so's you could *enjoy* it, Buck. They sent us on a *mission*. I'm really the one in charge and they want me to find out what's going on."

Skane snorted, "All right. What's going on, if you're so smart?"

Longarm sighed and said, "I'm trying to find out. I got a line on one prospector who vanished for certain after wiring home he'd struck color. That's more to go on than the vaguely worded complaint about gents who could have been carried off by goblins or just moved on to other parts. Mining men have restless feet as carry them off on the winds of rumor. But I've a name and with any luck a filed claim to work on now. I'm meeting kin of the missing man in town tonight. That's why you have to stay out here again, like it or not."

"I don't like it for shit," Skane said. "I've a good notion to quit and head back to Texas."

"I wish you would," said Longarm, truthfully.

But the Texican said he was going into Pot Luck to get laid instead, the spoilsport.

That gave Longarm all the time he needed to doctor more dynamite sticks with gold leaf and set them aside. He wasn't ready to use them, yet.

Knowing nobody was working the Fordham claim he'd just bought, and seeing old Goldberg hardly ever came up for air, Longarm capped and fused another end-to-end chain along the base of the unworked face.

Then, nosey parkers be damned, and having the time on his hands, Longarm wheeled more tailings downgrade to bury the same, idly wondering if he really needed to go through all this bullshit, since nobody else seemed interested.

There were other such claims, some of them being worked for pay dirt, stretching all the way south to the narrow-guage and, upslope, on other outcrops. Nell Fordham had said the smart money boys in Pot Luck had said there was little point in trying this far north of the few serious lodes that were already being worked. Pot Luck seemed slated to be another flash in the pan. There were more of those than the other kind in these here hills.

So what was behind all that mysterious skulduggery he was supposed to be investigating? Pot Luck would never add up to another Virginia City or Leadville. It figured to end up more like Gregory Gulch, where too many cooks had shared a modest broth. You had to sew up all the lodes where the lodes were modest in size and scattered if you wanted to rival the moguls of Virginia City or Leadville.

"That's likely the plan," Longarm told the crushed granite he was smoothing in place over dynamite. He nodded and added, "All we have to do is find out who's consolidating scattered small claims into one bigger mining company, then ask the son of a bitch what he's been up to!"

It seemed to take forever, but Buchanan T. Skane saved himself from the dreadful fate Longarm had in store for him by getting back before sundown, grinning like a shit-eating dog.

Longarm expected the beefy blond pest to brag on having had Greek Gloria three ways. But that wasn't it. Skane said, "You'll never guess what I just heard. My old drinking buddy, Goldberg, turned up at the assay office with fair to middling gold quartz in his hot little hands! Can you believe it?"

Longarm said, "Now that you mention it he did blast not long after you left for town. I wasn't paying much attention. Never noticed him mucking all that much."

Skane said, "He never. Old Jew could see right off there was cold in his blasted ore. Ran into town with some prime samples. I wasn't there. They were talking about it in the saloon. But it seems you could make out the gold in the quartz with your naked-ass eye! Ain't that a bitch?"

Longarm had to smile. But he soberly declared, "Well, hell, the man was drilling for *gold*, wasn't he? I take it he's still celebrating in the Crystal Palace?"

Skane shook his head and said, "Not hardly. Some of the boys wanted to celebrate him. But nobody's seen him since he danced a Jew hornpipe out front of the assay office. He's likely celebrating with other Jews somewhere. He'll likely be along directly, though. Don't sound smart to leave a proven claim unguarded. Nobody can jump Goldberg's, seeing he's got it on file with the government. But they were talking in town about high-graders. They's the thieves who steal gold nuggets and such out of a mine when nobody's looking, right?"

Longarm said, "That's about the size of it. Ore has to be pretty rich to tempt high-graders. Hardly pays to risk your life for a few cents at a time."

"Who's to say how rich old Goldberg's strike might be?" asked Skane, and Longarm bit his tongue, since he hadn't been there when the older man had likely felt like coming in his bib overalls.

The picture made Longarm feel shitty, even though he hadn't been the one who'd helped poor Goldberg salt his own try hole. He didn't dare tell such a loose cannon about that gold leaf. He had no call to, even if Skane had been more sensible. At this stage of the game nobody else had any need to know and he was having enough of a time acting surprised.

Leaving Skane to guard both their own try holes until he got back, Longarm walked back to town where, sure enough, Risa Ferrier sat waiting for him in a lobby chair, jumping to her feet with a "yoo-hoo" as Longarm came in from the gloaming outside. So he just steered her on into the dining room as she asked if he'd found out anything about her brother.

He seated her as he replied, "Not direct. But a picture may be emerging from the mists."

He didn't tell her what an ominous picture he had in mind as he took his own seat and signaled that same waitress, who looked worn down to a nub but was trying to keep a game face to the world as she limped.

After giving her their orders, Longarm told the sister of the missing Jacques Ferrier, "It's possible your brother was . . . bought out. Somebody may be trying to consolidate all the outcrop claims into one under the rule of apex. That's when you shut down all but your adit closer to the tip of the underground ore complex and set up some serious mining. You need a big single lode to finance such a deal."

She said she didn't understand.

He said, "Few folk do, Miss Risa. Only half the riches under the earth get extracted as minerals, if that much. Take my word on this because you'd fall asleep if I tried to explain in depth, but they do tell a tale of a young so-called investor who arrived in Virginia with less than a thousand dollars of his own to put down on silver futures and left a month later as a multimillionaire. He never got dirt under his fingernails in the process, neither."

"How is that possible?" she gasped.

He said, "I just told you it was. Because it is. Individual lodes of medium-grade ore can be bought at one price. Consolidated lodes making up the roots of a mountain range can be sold at another. There's a world of wheeling and dealing on the stock market before anybody mines all that much. Think of that old shell game with mountains as the shells and peas of gold, silver and such. Don't try to understand all the wheels within the wheels. Just take my word it looks as if some big wheel is out to wind up with the whole cuckoo clock."

Their weary little waitress brought their suppers. Longarm's home fries were overdone. He didn't say anything.

Risa's were nigh raw but she didn't say anything and Longarm could tell the waitress was grateful. He felt more kindly towards both gals as she tottered off.

Risa said, "They're overworking that poor child!" and Longarm said he'd noticed. He figured their waitress was around twenty but one of those naturally petite little things who never filled out until they'd had a kid, after which all bets were off. Professor Darwin had explained that aspect of evolution, too. He'd allowed there'd be fewer ugly middle-aged women if so many didn't look tolerable when they were young.

The more aristocratic Risa was asking him where her brother might be if he'd simply sold his claim.

Longarm didn't want to cross that bridge before they had to. He told her, "We want to find out if he *staked* a claim, where it might have been and who he might have sold it to before we worry about that, Miss Risa."

She didn't seem satisfied with that. He added, "Men can move about like Mexican jumping beans when they get to chasing one rainbow after another. We want to find out where he was, here in Pot Luck, before we even try to guess where he might have gone."

They finished their supper in no time because in truth neither wanted it to end. Once it had, Longarm had no choice but to pay the tab, surprise the waitress with a fair tip and escort Risa back into the lobby, allowing it had been swell talking to her.

She demured, "It's still so early and we've still so much to talk about. Do you think they might . . . object if I was to invite you up to my room for just a little while, Canada?"

Longarm replied, "It's been my experience that when you don't say nothing at the desk, they seldom say anything to you."

And that was how things worked out.

Chapter 11

Longarm had advised young squirts like Henry how easy it was to spoil what seemed a sure thing with the wrong remark when nerves were atingle. It was most often the gal, with more confounded feelings, who could shy like a spooked pony at a surprisingly dumb remark. But nobody enjoyed having the feelings they'd exposed splashed with the ice water of unconsidered observations about their inner selves. So Longarm felt a surprised thrill of resentment up in Risa's room when she coyly asked, as she poured cognac from a carpetbag into hotel tumblers, how often he'd waltzed past a hotel desk, up to a lady's room.

Still seated on the end of her bed, where she'd invited him to sit, Longarm wearily replied, "Not as often as I've often wanted, being a natural man. Would you like me to leave, now?"

She turned with a cognac in each hand to gasp, "*Mon Dieu*, what have I said to make you so angry, Canada?"

With a weary smile, he accepted the tumbler she was holding out and replied, "Not angry. Disappointed, Miss Risa. If I wanted to play kid games I'd scout up a kid, and it was your own grand notion to invite me up here. It was you who suggested we might have supper this evening, and as I recall, it was you who came up to me in the first place. I never forced my fool self on you."

She sat down beside him, soothingly saying, "I know. Can't you take a little joke?"

He said, "Jokes about us raging bulls chasing you helpless things until you catch us get less amusing after a time. Where in the U.S. Constitution does it say gals get to call it flirting when they give a man the eye, but they get to call a man a sex fiend if he even returns one wink?"

She flushed and looked away as she murmured, "Touché! One developes rude habits in my position, Canada."

"What might your position be, Miss Risa?" he replied, sipping at his cognac to find it four star.

She said, "My brother and I were left a family business to conduct, and guess who got, how you say, stuck with running it? I have had to watch my step with men who came calling with all sorts of propositions and only half of them were after . . . my body. When one never knows what a man is after, one has one's guard up at all times and, sometimes, a little high, *n'est-ce pas*?"

"I ain't after your family business," said Longarm, dryly.

She laughed and said, "Flattery will get you everything. I've already been seduced by a man who was after our money. Fortunately, neither Jacques nor myself alone can sign over the entailed inheritance. I shall spare you the tale of the *très formidable* argument we had over Jacque's desire to go into the telephone business. Suffice it to say he met an inventor at his club who claimed to have invented the telephone."

"Was his name Alexander Graham Bell?" asked Longarm.

She sighed wearily and replied, "*Mais non*, it was Chambrun, I believe. I found his story less convincing when Jacques brought him home with him."

Longarm smiled thinly and declared, "That makes two

of us, Miss Risa. It's long been my clear understanding that old Alexander Graham Bell unveiled that invention at the 1876 Exposition in Philadelphia. Didn't you all hear about that up Canada way, Mr. Bell being Canadian and all?"

She sighed and said, "The one Jacques invested his own money in was an improved model. Perhaps it was. But they were unable to manufacture it with the Bell Telephone Company holding all those patents. As I told you earlier, I tried to talk Jacques out of this gold rush. As you see, I was not able to and . . . Are you some species of policeman, Canada?"

"What might have given you that grand notion?" Longarm asked with his best poker face.

She said, "It just occurred to me how . . . *investigative* you seem to have approached my brother's disappearance. I never would have thought to ask your Bureau of Mines about a possible claim they have on file. Not one person I spoke to earlier suggested that, including the town marshal when I went to him for help. Does not it strike you as odd that a mining man I took for a fellow Canadian would seem more professional than a man they pay to uphold the law in Pot Luck?"

Longarm shrugged and said, "Mayhaps they don't pay him enough. If the truth be known, half the lawmen out our way are just natural bullies willing to work cheap. Last I'd heard, they made Ben Thompson the city marshal of Austin and everybody knows he's a crazy-mean drunk."

He sipped more cognac and loftily conceded, "I'm likely smarter and more curious by nature than the local law."

It got easy to feel lofty as one sipped four-star cognac up in a lady's hotel room.

Before it could be determined how lofty she was feeling, there came a soft tapping on the hall door.

The two of them exchanged puzzled looks. Risa got up

and went to the door. It was their waitress from downstairs. She ducked inside and shut the door after her, gasping, "Oh, thank your lucky stars you ain't in turpentine yet!"

Risa blinked, "Turpentine?"

The little gimpy gal with mouse-colored hair and a not-bad-looking but sort of chinless face said, "Mortal turpentine, ma'am. I heard the marshal talking to the desk clerk downstairs as I was getting off just now. They call me Molly, Molly Boone, when they notice me at all. Nobody was paying attention to me as I was changing into my street duds in the cloak room behind the desk. That's when I heard the marshal say he had you on a charge of mortal turpentine if he wanted."

Longarm said, "I suspect moral turpitude is the charge he had in mind, Miss Molly. Might you know what time they're fixing to raid us?"

She said, "I ain't dead certain they mean to. Marshal Ellison said he *could* arrest you on mortal turpentine any time he had a mind to. Only I got the expression he might be holding it over you-all, like a threat, when and if he got word from Mr. Prince."

They both asked who Mr. Prince might be.

Molly said, "I don't know. I keep hearing gents whisper about him as I wait tables downstairs. Like I said, nobody notices me much. But I get the expression Mr. Prince runs things here in Pot Luck."

"Why might this M'sieur Prince hold ill will against either of us?" asked Risa.

Molly said, "Not Mr. Canada, ma'am. *You*. Marshal Ellison said he was tired of you pestering him about something. When the desk clerk made a dirty remark about you having a man in your room, the marshal laughed dirty, too, and allowed Mr. Prince might be happy to hear that. I don't know whether they mean to bust in on you tonight or not. But I thought I ought to warn you!"

Risa put her hands on the younger gal's waifish shoulders to say, "This was most kind of you, Molly. *Mais pourquoi*? You do not know us. We owe you nothing. Why would you risk your position downstairs for us?"

Molly looked away and said, "Aw, it ain't such a grand job and you folk both . . . noticed me."

She turned back to meet Risa's eye as she added, "I ain't talking about the tip. I get tips all the time. You both smiled and thanked me when I brung your orders. I don't get smiled at often. I don't get *looked* at all that often."

Then she pulled away and said, "I gotta go. It ain't much of a job. But it is a job."

Risa hauled her in for a hug and let her go. As Molly ducked outside, Longarm rose, saying, "Better make that the both of us. I'll slip out the back way."

He reached in his denim jacket to fish out a folded envelope, not daring to pack his field notebook or other proper identification, and told her, "Let me have an address in Denver, Miss Risa. I'll contact you as soon as I learn anything."

She asked why on earth she'd want to go to Denver and he asked her, "Weren't you paying attention just now? The town law could be fixing to pick you up on a morals charge!"

She sniffed, "I haven't done anything immoral. He's decided I'm a pest because I keep asking him for the help he has the sworn duty to extend to me!"

Longarm said, "Miss Risa, he don't *want* to help you. I'm commencing to agree your brother could be in trouble. I want you safely out of Pot Luck before I have to worry about you, too!"

She said, "I won't leave until I find out what's become of Jacques!" She sounded as if she meant it.

Since life was so short, Longarm said, "All right. Let's get you packed and we'll *both* sneak out the back way."

She insisted, "I'm not going down to Denver, damn it!"

He said, "We've established that. I'm taking you to the recent camp of a respectable woman and her innocent children. I'll explain along the way. Let's get you packed and out of here!"

So they did, and when Marshal Ellison and his just recruited matrons busted in after midnight they found Theresa Ferrier's room empty.

Mr. Prince didn't like that at all when the bewildered marshal reported to him in the wee small hours.

Mr. Prince said, "I told you to take care of the problem, not to *compound* it, you blithering simp! What on earth possessed you to confide in that room clerk and those two whores? How in the devil are you ever going to dispose of her discreetly now that all those witnesses you were bright enough to confide in will recall you describing her as a pest?"

Ellison sniveled, "How was I to know that cuss called Canada might suspect I had my eye on him?"

"How indeed?" purred Mr. Prince, adding, "You, yourself, said he was a knock about hairpin who knows his way around the high country. It was you who told me about him turning the tables and staring down a very dangerous card shark last night. Did you really think to hang a morals charge on any man who can produce a straight flush out of thin air? I want you to find out more about this Canada Cooper, Marshal. That can't be his real name. Nobody who's never met up with bigger boos than Major Manson would turn his back on the same and walk away with his money. Men with that much nerve know they're good. Men don't know they're good until they've killed. More than once. Find out who the man called Canada might have killed."

"What about the gal?" asked Ellison.

Mr. Prince said, "Fuck the girl. If she'll have you. She'll still be there if and when we need to kill her."

"Hold on!" the marshal blanched. "Nobody never said nothing about me killing no woman! I ain't never killed a woman, Mr. Prince!"

The entity he actually worked for purred, "Try it. You'll

like it. But first, find out who Canada Cooper is. If he's the sort I suspect he is I may have use for him. So I don't want him arrested on any charge before I give the word."

"Not even if I catch him in bed with that pesky Canadian gal?" asked the town law.

"Not even if you catch him in bed with your own woman," Mr. Prince replied dryly, adding, "All bets are off if I catch him in bed with *my* woman, and, Marshal, don't ever tell me who you might or might not kill when and if I tell you to. I'm not going to say that again."

Marshal Ellison allowed he understood and let himself out of the dark and apparently deserted office, his flesh crawling as it always did after a private meeting with Mr. Prince.

The marshal wondered if Mr. Prince made everybody's flesh crawl. It wasn't the sort of question any one asked, if you knew what was good for you.

By the time Longarm had Risa out to that abandoned covered wagon, he'd explained how he'd bought the claim off of Nell Fordham, who was last seen headed to Kansas with her kids. Risa started to ask a dumb question and bit her tongue. She was learning how to best get along with the man she called Canada.

He lit an oil lamp and helped her up into the wagon fitted out as family quarters, saying, "Some of the bedding may smell gamey as they left it. There's clean linens and a heap of duds they left behind in the back. Like I told you coming over the reef, nobody else has any call to visit a claim they don't own and that ain't being worked. If anyone comes by, you're to tell them to see me or Buck, to the south, because we're the owners and you're just watching this wagon for us."

He climbed over a rumpled pile of quilts and such to rummage for a clean Mother Hubbard, saying, "There should be a sunbonnet, here, somewheres. If you change into 'em you ought to look close enough to the gal they're used to seeing hereabouts and, like I said, nobody has any call to come close for the time you'll be hiding out in plain sight here."

She asked how long they might hope to get away with such a brazen ploy. That was what she called a plan he thought right simple—a brazen ploy.

He said, "We should know within, say, forty-eight hours whether your big brother ever filed a claim in this mining district. If he never did, there's your answer. He ain't here because he's somewhere else."

She asked, "And if we discover Jacques filed a claim, Canada?"

He said, "Let's hope we don't. If we do, there ought to be a transfer of ownership and that will give us pinned down places and persons to go on. It ain't easy as some crooks think to jump a claim these days. Federal records leave a plain paper trail to follow."

She said, "You mean, if we find Jacques filed a claim, and someone else now holds it, we can assume the new owners did something vile to my poor brother?"

He said, "No. The claim could have changed hands, more than once, since your brother was last seen working it. Don't you want to wait until I leave before you unbutton all them buttons, Miss Risa?"

She asked, "*Pourquoi*? You were going somewhere?"

Longarm started to explain he and old Buck were bedded down to the south. Then he wondered why on earth any man would want to say a dumb thing like that. So he just trimmed the lamp and after a time they found their way to one another in the dark, by touch.

She sure touched good.

After that it seemed only natural to burrow into the covers together and to hell with clean linens. Neither Nell Fordham nor her kids had been all that disgusting and, as Longarm got going in the dark with Risa, the mingled body odors of two reasonably clean women didn't bother him at all. Albeit it felt sort of French when you studied on it.

But in truth, there was nothing all that depraved about the way Risa made love, as if they'd been to bed before, somewhere, sometime, and it sure felt swell to meet up again with such a warm-natured old pal.

Things happened that way, on all too rare occasions. He sensed it had happened before to her when she never commented on the wonder of it all and simply accepted miracles as they were intended.

He knew it was too good to last. He knew they could only risk it for a few short days at the most.

That was why he didn't want to stop when they came.

And why she didn't want him to.

Chapter 12

This wise old philosopher had written one time, in French, how once love had flown not even the lovers could say what all the fuss had been about. But Longarm felt it sure beat all how so many gals could have learned to screw so swell from other men who'd never meant all that much to them. Albeit, in fairness, Longarm was sore put to remember who might have taught him that corkscrew motion Risa found "*très intéressant*" dog-style.

Hence, by the cold sane light of dawn, Longarm had heard more than he'd ever wanted to about a failed marriage and a couple of long engagements that just hadn't panned out. He'd figured she'd meant those smoke signals she'd been sending with her eyes from the beginning.

Risa wanted to tag along for breakfast with him and old Buck. Longarm told her he didn't want to introduce her to old Buck, explaining, "I'm sure he means well but he's a pathetic poker player. So like I told you last night, it may be best if nobody sees you up close as you keep an eye on this claim. Let's see if we can find that sunbonnet and a clean Mother Hubbard as fits."

They could, and when he turned halfway south to his

pitched tent to wave, Risa waved back, looking enough like Nell Fordham at a distance to pass casual inspection.

Over at their nearby claim, his untrustworthy sidekick was polishing off biscuits and beans with reheated coffee. As Longarm joined him, Old Buck grinned up to say, "I was wondering where you were. I thought you said your poor Nelly was off to Kansas."

Longarm said, "The kids have gone on. Final transfer papers may take some time to clear. Ought to have somebody keeping an eye on all that other gear and we don't want stray kids poking around in that other try hole. I asked the lady yonder to hang around and keep an eye on things 'til we hire some help."

"When do we get to hire some help?" asked Skane, adding, "Even when you fake most of the work it's a pain in the ass to be stuck out here with a whole boomtown a couple of furlongs away."

Longarm said, "It would look suspicious for prospectors with an unproven claim to take on help for day wages. I figure on striking color in a day or so. Once we do, we both get to loll about like big shots whilst our hired crew drills and blasts for publication."

Skane frowned thoughtfully and asked, "You have the magic powers to hit pay dirt anytime it suits your fancy? I've always wished my cock was an inch or so longer. Anything you can do about that?"

Longarm laughed and hunkered down to build some fresh coffee, having shared beans and canned peaches with Risa earlier.

The big blond Texican pouted, "You don't mean to tell me, huh? Have it your way. Did you see old Goldberg in town last night?"

Longarm said, "I wasn't looking for him. Ain't that him over yonder? Hunkered by his own fire with his back to us?"

Skane said, "Not hardly. I strolled over at daybreak, meaning to ask if he had any more white lightning to spare.

102

Cocksucker with his back turned our way like his shit don't stink waved a ten-guage Greener at me and yelled the property was private and posted."

Longarm went on rinsing out stale grounds with canteen water as he thought about that. He waited until he had the fresh pot on the coals before he got back to his feet and decided, "We'll see about that. Cover me from the far side of the buckboard with that Winchester Yellow Boy we picked up in town."

Not waiting for Skane to get moving, since he would or he wouldn't prove worth shit in a pinch, Longarm strode south along the footpath until, sure enough, the stranger who'd been hunkered with his back to them got up and slowly turned with a sawed-off shotgun at port, calling out, "This here's the Coleson claim and no trespassin' is allowed!"

Longarm kept coming, calling back, "I ain't a trespasser. I'm neighborhood. On good terms with old Moe Goldberg!"

The surly stranger with the ten-guage street sweeper called back in as unkind a tone, "That old Jew don't hold this claim no more. It's the property of Doc Coleson and he told us to keep things just the way they was out here."

The *us* explained the apparent eyes in the back of the guard's head. His partner, covering approaches from their north, remained hidden from view to back the standing man's play as Longarm stopped where he was to smile uncertainly and call back, "Do tell? When did this all happen and how come old Goldberg never said toad squat to us about a sellout?"

The burly gent with the Greener shrugged and said, "I wasn't there. I never met the old Jew. I was hired by Doc Coleson last night, after he'd bought Goldberg out. Doc's orders are to just keep things the way they are. Preserved in amber, as he puts it."

Longarm said, "It's his claim, in amber or producing

103

pay dirt. So let me guess. This Doc Coleson's sitting on a proven claim with a view to reselling it for a modest profit, right?"

The guard posted by the new owner asked, "How should I know? Do I work in Doc Coleson's fucking drugstore? Like I said, we just work here. And you don't."

Longarm laughed lightly and called, "That sounds reasonable. They call me Canada Cooper. My pard would be Buck Skane. I just put on fresh coffee and it's Arbuckle brand if you'd care for some."

There came a low muble of conversation meant to be private. Then the only one in view called back, "That's right neighborly of you, Canada. But we got orders. So thanks just the same."

Longarm nodded and went back to his own claim. Skane came from behind the buckboard without the Yellow Boy, observing, "You let him crawfish you."

Longarm said, "No, I didn't. I allowed a man to do the job he was hired to do. Nobody has call to jump another owner's claim."

"What do you think they done to that old Jew?" Skane demanded, adding, "It's plain as the warts on a toad's ass. Old Goldberg turned up at the assay office with some color and now he's no longer with us. It's like them others, carried off by the goblins right after they hit pay dirt!"

He hunkered down by the fire, adding, "I was just getting used to old Moe, too. He wasn't such a bad neighbor, for a Jew."

Longarm said, "Let's duck down in the try hole. We want those birds to tell that druggist we left them alone and worked our own claim today."

So that was what they did, setting off a blast that brought the second guard into view to the south and inspired Risa to give a pretty fair imitation of Nell Fordham staring from the north.

Then they mucked for a spell and Longarm said he had to run their ore samples into the assay office.

Skane pouted, "What the hell for? We both know we've just been blowing the same loose dirt around and there was never a dime's worth of shit in it to begin with!"

Longarm said, "You know that and I know that but *they* ain't supposed to know that. Would you rather we really drilled into solid rock an inch at a time for worthless ore to assay?"

The towhead allowed that when you put things that way there seemed to be method in Longarm's madness. But he insisted, "I want to go into town where the lights are bright and the women ain't!"

He waved to the north to grumble, "It's all very well for you to guard all this useless rock with your heart and soul. You got your own supply of pussy within easy walking distance."

Then he grinned dirty and asked, "I don't suppose you'd be willing to offer sloppy seconds to a pal?"

Longarm said, "I don't think she'd go for it. You know how romantic some married women can be. But I'll tell you what. With those hired guns on guard to the south and old . . . Nell camped just up the way, it ought to be safe to leave this site unguarded after dark. Long as everybody at any distance can see it's being worked by day."

Skane said, "Now you're talking! Ain't a fucking thing out here worth stealing, when you get right down to it!"

So they agreed Skane would stay visibly on guard until sundown and then feel free to see if Greek Gloria still loved him. Longarm left by broad day, albeit late in the afternoon, carrying coals to Newcastle or, in this case, country rock to be assayed for mineral content.

He managed to hide his disappointment when another day's hard toil panned out as eight percent granite and twenty percent quartz, period. From the assay office he ankled over to the Western Union to see if the Bureau of Mines had any light to shed on the comings and goings of Jacques Ferrier.

They did. It sure helped to have the Denver District Court backing you when you asked some simple questions.

The answers were less simple. Risa's missing brother had indeed recorded a proven claim of blossom rock or decomposed quartz laced with native gold you could separate nigh untreated with mercury and yielding an estimated sixty dollars a ton, or just over the edge into where it paid you to hire three shifts, put in power drills and produce some damned tonnage.

But according to the Bureau of Mines, old Jacques had sold his claim in an outcrop, up the mountain from that more popular reef, to yet another businessman in town for twenty-five hundred dollars. Longarm made a note of the new owner's name, who'd described himself as a livery owner. Twenty-five hundred was a modest offer for a marginally profitable gold mine. So the livery man had most likely bought cheap to sell dear. Just where Jacques Ferrier might have gone with his modest profits remained a mystery.

As he was leaving the telegraph office, Longarm was startled to see old Moe Goldberg coming in, looking a tad bushed but otherwise in good health.

Longarm stopped his former neighbor to introduce himself and comment on Goldberg's good fortune. Adding in an uncertain tone, "We, ah, missed you out around your claim, Mr. Goldberg."

The hitherto sullen loner grinned like a kid without a care in the world and said, "What can I tell you? After you've been pounding rock for a while, ass feels fine. I'd forgotten how fine it could feel. So we sent out for extra help and had a party. Now I have to wire the wife and tell her I'm coming home with bells on!"

Longarm laughed and said, "My sincere congratulations to the both of you. I take it you got a good price for your claim?"

Goldberg winked and said, "Confidential, I was ready to quit when I came up with a little color. I've been in this game a while. So between you and me I'm not sure who's getting fucked. Could be I'm walking away from a bonanza. Could be I just sold an anomaly. That's what geologists call a brief concentration in a crack, an anomaly. Confidential, there was something about those samples that didn't seem kosher. The color should have been concentrated in the quartz. It was all through the granite. If I hadn't drilled that face myself, I'd wonder about salting. But how could a man salt his own claim without noticing?"

"It does sound difficult," Longarm replied, allowing himself to laugh before adding, "This is none of my beeswax, but seeing I'm working the same reef, could you suggest a price me and old Buck ought to hold out for?"

Goldberg said, "I was offered twenty-five hundred. I took it. What I hit would have cost them a hundred thousand had I been sure. Since I'm not, mazel tov and I'm getting too old for gold mining. I promised the wife this was my last grab for the gold ring and I meant it!"

They shook on that and parted friendly, Longarm mulling over the numbers in his head. They were modest numbers when you considered what a man could make out this way with any luck. But they added up to more than most men ever saw when the average going price for common labor was no more than a dollar a day.

Goldberg had netted as much for his few months of back-breaking toil as an executive with a college degree might take home in three years. But on the other hand, they said Silver Dollar Tabor wore hundred-dollar shirts and kept both a wife and mistress in high style. So that was what Mr. Karl Marx was writing all those manifestos about. Longarm had never come up with a way to assure everyone a square deal and he doubted anybody ever would. Some old boys were doomed to work themselves to death at starvation wages whilst others got born with silver spoons to lick.

It was the ones born poor who meant to die rich, or *else*, who caused most of the trouble a lawman was expected to worry about.

When he rejoined Risa Ferrier out at the Fordham camp he told her what he'd found out about her missing brother's claim and added, "It looks as if somebody feeling slick has lesser lights buying up scattered claims with a view to someday owning and mayhaps selling the whole field to one of those big syndicates like Meyer Guggenheim runs."

As she whipped up French crêpes, or fancy flapjacks, over the coals of her night fire the Canadian gal said, "I know Jacques would never sell a gold mine for twenty-five hundred dollars. Not even if it wasn't worth as much! Can't you see somebody forced him to sell, or perhaps they forged a transfer of ownership after they . . . did something vile to my poor daydreaming brother?"

He assured her it was as likely Jacques had taken a modest profit and, like Goldberg, moved on. He was lying, of course. Goldberg would have held out for the going medium price of a hundred thousand for a *proven* but undeveloped claim. Men who dealt in gold futures thought big and if they didn't have the money to play mining mogul, they played poker. The mastermind, if there was a mastermind, meant to spend his hundred or so thousand cornering all the claims in the field, paying front men to hold his growing monopoly as modestly worked or unworked properties until . . . ?

That was a good question.

The missing Jacques Ferrier's sister posed a flaw in any mastermind's reasoning when she asked, as they supped, "Would not all these bogus transfers to small investors lead like the roads to Rome, in the end, to the one great budding baron all of them are fronting for?"

Longarm said, "*In time* is a spoon that can really stir the pot. I was reading in the *Scientific American* how, someday, after everybody keeps all business records on standard forms, with typewriters and mayhaps them trick index cards with holes punched along the edges, it might only take months instead of years for bank examiners and treasury accountants to follow a paper trail back to its beginnings. But today ain't someday and by the time you shuffle drawers full of business records like cards in a deck, back and forth with most of the deals only made up, in longhand, by a law clerk who may or may not have known what he or she was asked to transfer from one sheet of paper to another . . ."

She insisted, "*Oui, mon cher*, but as I said, all roads lead to Rome in the end, *hein*?"

He said, "Not as you can prove before a judge and jury possessed of no more than brilliant brains. So what prosecuting attorney is about to charge some wheeling-and-dealing mining magnate, way down your road to Rome, with having bought up a claim here and an option there off some other innocent soul listed as the third, fourth or seventy-seventh owner since an earlier owner may or may not have met with foul play? I fear this Mr. Prince they whisper about, if there's any such cuss, will have covered his tracks under a blizzard of swirling paper before it comes time to go public as one big mining outfit, merge with some other big mining outfit or just sell out at a whooping profit."

"Then what are we to do?" she sobbed.

He moved around the fire to take her in his arms as he told her, "*We* don't have to do nothing, little darling. First let me kiss your tears away and, come morning, me and old Buck will see about baiting a hook for our Mr. Prince."

Chapter 13

Way later, in the wee small hours with both Buck and Risa asleep and no signs of life from the claim to their south, Longarm waited until he was down in the try hole to strike a match and light the oil lantern.

He capped and fused another chain of dynamite sticks, with a couple of them wrapped in gold leaf, meaning to chum the fish pond some before he put out serious bait.

Then, mindful of the reservations expressed by the experienced Goldberg, he selected hunks of milky quartz from his first wheelbarrow load to carefully balance atop the doctored sticks along the base of the face and gently buried them that way with other dust and debris.

He'd had no call to explain his actions to either Buck or Risa. Neither had reason to know and secrets were easier to keep when you didn't have anything to hide.

Next morning he and Buck went through the motions, blasting a little after noon and waving back, both ways, as they mucked. That afternoon Longarm heard better news at the assay office. Some of his quartz had yielded traces of color to the acid test.

The acid test for gold was simple. Gold dissolved in *aqua regia* but no other acid. So anything that looked like gold and refused to dissolve in sulfuric or nitric acids but melted like sugar into *aqua regia* had to be gold.

Aqua regia was a wicked mixture of hydrochloric and nitric acids. Nitic acid alone would eat the shit out of most anything but gold or platinum. Mixed with milder hydrochloric acid it was something else and accounted for all that chloride ore up that way. Natural sulfuric acid produced all that green copper ore. Professors stayed up nights worrying about such shit.

The old pro at the assay office told "Canada Cooper" he had color worth serious drilling. So Longarm allowed he was going to the Crystal Palace to celebrate. It wasn't the old gent who ran the assay office who sent word to an agent of Mr. Prince. It was a bottle washer in the back with a taste for the finer things in life.

As Canada Cooper, Longarm didn't brag right out on striking color. He got the barkeep aside and confided he was in the market for a drilling crew willing to work cheap.

The barkeep said, "This one old boy laid off up Leadville way as a labor agitator has run up quite a tab on us, Canada. How much are you willing to pay?"

"Dollar a shift, apiece, for two good men willing to drive that steel on down and hold off on the rights of the laboring man. They'll be working one short shift a day."

The barkeep said, "I'll pass it on. They might not go for it. You ain't asking 'em to herd cows down yonder under the mountain, you know."

Longarm said he knew what it felt like to drive steel, having just done some. He added he couldn't afford the going rates and they could take his offer or pay for their drinks some other way.

The barkeep allowed he could try. Longarm knew he'd round up some barflies willing to work for a cowhand's base pay. He wanted them to resent it. Workers who felt loyalty to a boss didn't talk behind his back as readily.

Over in the corner, Major Manson was shooting daggers with his eyes. So Longarm wandered over to a far wall where a good-looking but dead-eyed henna redhead was dealing faro. She had others bucking the tiger as they stared down the front of her low-cut black velvet bustier. Gals dressed that scandalous could get arrested in some towns. Longarm never threw pocket jingle away on faro when he didn't have to. But he enjoyed the show a spell as he nursed his beer.

A familiar voice to his left said, "Great minds run in the same dirty channels. They call her Rosemary. She packs a Harrington Richardson point thirty-two. Understand you boys struck color this afternoon."

Longarm turned to smile down at the older Zip Finny as Longarm allowed he might have produced enough gold to fill a tooth, as long as it wasn't a big tooth.

The general store owner said, "Reminds me of the one time I tried my hand at panning, over in Denver when they called it Cherry Creek. It was like eating peanuts. You know how hard it is to stop eating peanuts once you start? I *knew* I was making less than a Chinese laundryman for a hard day's work, but it was *gold*, by damn, there for the swishing if you swished enough fucking sand, hour after hour."

Longarm said, "I take it you ain't into mining investments, like so many others up this way?"

Finny shook his graying head to reply, "Learned long ago the best way to show a profit from mining is to sell the picks and shovels. You ever see that famous tombstone in Central City, the one as reads: Here lies the body of D. C. Oates killed for starting the Pikes Peak hoax?"

Longarm chuckled and said, "I have. But I heard it was a fake."

Zip Finny shrugged and said, "It's the sentiment that counts. For every one of you birds who strikes color there's mayhaps a thousand who limp on home flat broke, if they're lucky. Lots of tombstones out our way tell the simple truth. But I've never heard-tell of a man going broke selling tools and provisions."

Longarm said, "I noticed. We're going to be needing more dynamite, by the way."

When Finny said, "I know," Longarm asked, "Who told you? I just found out myself."

The older man shrugged and replied, "Who told me Miss Rosemary, yonder, packs a gun and don't put out? Word gets around fast in a mining camp, like cigar smoke, with nobody able to rightly say who lit that first cigar."

Longarm knew that was the simple truth, so he didn't pursue it. He asked Finny, "What do they say about this Mr. Prince I hear so much about?"

The merchant easily replied, "What's the true story of D. C. Oates, if there ever was a D. C. Oates? You hear all sorts of shit about some shady mining man called Mr. Prince. Some of them might be true. I don't see how *all* of them could be."

"What are the things you don't buy, seeing anything seems possible?" asked Longarm.

Finny said, "That's easy. Some say it ain't wise to cross Mr. Prince. They intimate bad things happen to those who cross Mr. Prince. They say he runs things up this way."

"You hear such tales in most every town, large or small," Longarm observed.

Zip Finny said, "I know. So where might our Mr. Prince be if he's running things? Nobody's running *me*. Nobody's ever *tried* to run me. If the mysterious cuss *was* running me, what might he *want* from me?"

Longarm said, "You likely don't have anything he wants, if he's here at all. They say the bogeyman is particular about the naughty boys he carries off to bogey land."

Finny shrugged and said, "I ain't sure I buy the bogeyman, neither. Have you ever wondered who *they* might be? The ones you hear about when you hear '*they* say,' or '*they* might do' this or that?"

113

Longarm said, "You may be right," hoping he wasn't. For unless there *was* a bogeyman around there, someplace, he might never figure out where Jacques Ferrier and those other missing folk had wound up.

Having finished his main chores at the saloon, Longarm dropped by the restaurant where Molly Boone waited tables to grab a bite and see if she'd overheard anything new before he headed home.

She had. As she took his order she murmured, "Can't talk here. I'm off early tonight to tend a candlelight vigil for a gal who died. Meet me at First Congregationalist at ten and walk me home natural. Like we met there by accident. Gotta go, now."

She left for the kitchen with his order before he could say yes or no. On reflection he didn't see how he could say no. So he dawdled at his supper, dropped by other saloons to see if he could get the temper of a town he didn't really know, and asked directions to the First Congregationalist.

The small neatly whitewashed frame church was up towards the north end of Pot Luck, where some of the best housing was, albeit none of the housing in the new mining camp was all that imposing.

The front door hung open despite the hour and the cooler night air. The interior was softly lit. Others were drifting for the door. Longarm asked an older gent if that might be where they were holding services for Miss Violet Brown, a name he made up from whole cloth.

The older man shook his head and said, "Young cleaning woman called Kitty Flynn. Died of consumption the other night. They say she was a Roman Catholic but there's no Catholic church in town yet and the Reverend Ashton is being a sport about it. He's agreed with her Papist friends to shoot for an R.C. send-off."

Longarm thanked the old-timer, let him go on in and settle down, then mounted the steps and strolled in to spy a coffin down the aisle by the simple altar. A bare cross hung on the whitewashed wall above the altar. White candles illuminated the gal lying dead in the coffin. She'd been too young. It hadn't been fair. But that was consumption for you. They called it the white plague. The young cleaning woman in the pine box looked to be made of the same white tallow as the candles lit for her. The white plague sucked the life out of you from inside, like one of those vampires that Irish writer, Mr. La Shan, described.

What the older man had said about the sort of Irish-looking gal in the pine box fit with what Longarm had heard about the Congregationalists, a middle-of-the-road Calvinist sect. Their ministers, like Jewish rabbis, were hired by their self-governing congregations and allowed some leeway.

It still seemed sporting to take in a departed soul belonging to another faith entire and send her off according to her own lights.

So when he found Molly Boone talking in a corner to a sky pilot who looked something like Abe Lincoln, Longarm moved to join them and wasn't too surprised by the friendly smile and firm handshake of the Reverend Ashton, who allowed his friends called him Ash.

Molly proved herself a natural actress by acting surprised to see Longarm and introducing him as one of her nicer customers from that restaurant. She said she hadn't known "Canada" had known poor Kitty.

Longarm said, "I was only introduced to her as we shopped in the same general store. I helped her with a heavy load as far as her hired hack. I could see she was sickly. Never suspected she was *that* sick, though."

Old Ash excused himself to join others coming in to pay their respects. Molly said, "Isn't he nice? Says he knows Catholics and Jews use the same psalm about green pastures and means to read it over Kitty tomorrow. They're letting her rest in their Protestant churchyard 'til such time as someone might want to move her somewheres else. What do you call it when you bury outsiders in your own churchyard, Mr. Cooper?"

He said, "Christian. Call me Canada. You said you had something to tell me about Mr. Prince?"

She said, "Let's say you're escorting me home. My place is a ways to the south."

Nobody questioned them as they left together. As she took his arm, Molly said, "Marshal Ellison was telling this gent I don't know how Miss Risa had stopped pestering him and might have left town. Then he said Mr. Prince had said to leave you and Mr. Skane to ripen on the vine a spell and do something about that fucking Swede. It wasn't my idea to use such words, Canada. That's what Mr. Price called the poor man."

"Do you know who such a Swede might be?" asked Longarm.

She didn't. So all he knew as they parted out front of her tar-paper-and-frame cottage was that some fucking Swede was in a serious fix.

Parting was more awkward than sweet sorrow. She never said it, but a man could tell when a gal expected him to kiss her good night.

A man who kissed one gal good night when he was fixing to go to bed with another was a damned fool telling himself he was a sly dog. So he just shook with her and headed on home to Risa.

He told Risa some of what he'd seen and heard in town. They agreed it hadn't told them much about her brother Jacques and asking around town for a fucking Swede was only likely to make matters worse.

So they climbed into the wagon to undress and make up for the hours perforce spent apart. They were at that swell sweet stage where it felt like coming home to the most wonderful girl in the world who hadn't started to nag you, yet. Old Risa had even turned out a good sport about his half-ass beard. She said she'd always wondered what it might be like to be raped by the Wild Man from Borneo.

He figured, with any luck, they had to the end of the month before she said a man with any respect for a woman would try to look more civilized and either strike gold or get a regular job for Gawd's sake.

That was how come they called those first golden nights in bed a honeymoon. When they lasted more than a month it was time to consider hanging on to a gal. But he had it on good authority that when you did they generally left you for another man eight or nine years down the line.

But what the hell, with any luck he'd crack the case before then.

Next morning, breaking fast with Buchanan T. on their own claim, the towheaded Texican said, "You never told me your Nell was a French Canadian gal, pard."

"How did you figure that?" asked Longarm, feeling as if a big gray cat had got up to turn around twice and settle back down in his guts.

The Texican cheerfully replied, "She told me, when I went over last night to see if there was anything I could . . . do for her."

Longarm said, "Don't do that again. I mean it. You and me ain't going to put on our usual act today. I mean to hire some drillers with drinking problems and really drill into the face this time, to bring down fresh ore in front of witnesses. You go on and take the day off, if you've a mind to. But stay the hell away from . . . Nell Fordham."

He got to his feet, adding, "Like the Indian chief said, I have spoken."

Then he strode back up the reef to ask Risa why she hadn't told him the blond oaf had been pestering her.

Risa sighed and said, "The tone of your voice at the moment is why. Buck was no problem. He only wanted to fuck me and don't you think I'm capable of fending off eager pups?"

"That's neither here nor there. You should have told me," Longarm insisted.

She insisted, "You're being possessive. I don't like it, even though or perhaps because you have nothing to feel jealous about. I didn't tell for the simple reason it was not important. I was afraid you'd strike such an attitude, and I'll not have men fighting over me as if I were a rag doll!"

He said, "It ain't that I'm jealous. You'd have to be a man to understand. When a man has a pard, the pard ain't supposed to pussyfoot around behind his back. It's understood your possibles, your tobacco and your gal should be left alone by a pard, and there's other things that fool Texican has done to rile me."

She chortled, "You *are* jealous! I admit I find it flattering. But I warn you, Canada, I shall not have the two of you fighting like school boys over me!"

"Don't worry. You won't," said Longarm, soberly.

He'd meant he meant to lay down the law to a junior deputy. But as he strode off for town, she made the sign of the cross and sighed, "*Merde, alors*, not again!"

Chapter 14

Longarm was back from town a little after ten with their mules and a pair of Cousin Jacks who answered to Drake and Trevor and swore they'd learned their craft in the Cornish tin mines. They were both dark and swarthy. Drake was a short and stocky. Trevor was another Abe Lincoln with rail-splitter arms. They both got right to work with their shirts off.

Buchanan T. watched a spell before deciding all that work was giving him a thirst. He asked Longarm for the wherewithal to go to town. It seemed early to start drinking but Longarm didn't want professionals to hear kid questions from a man who was supposed to have been working the same face all that time.

You saw why Cousin Jacks were in such demand as hard-rock miners, even resentful labor agitators with dreadful thirsts; when you watched these old pros you could see they knew what they were doing. Taking turns without missing more than one or two out of a hundred strokes, they made steel ring loud as hell against the stone. Standing well back, Longarm was reminded of that work song boast that went:

Ain't no hammer
Under this mountain
That can ring like mine, boys
That can ring like mine!
They can hear my hammer
All over this valley
All the way to the jail, boys
All the way to the jail!

Longarm figured Trevor and Drake could be heard at least as far as the the first houses east of the reef. But that wasn't the point. The point was that *they*, not he or Skane, were drilling deep into the face.

They drilled so good it wasn't long after the time Longarm had set those four-flushing blasts under loose rubble before they all agreed it was time to set the charges, twenty-five in all. Longarm did so by planting sticks wrapped in gold leaf in all but a cornet trio of drill holes, where no quartz marbled the darker gray granite.

Like a shell game operator or a three-card monte dealer, Longarm seemed to just fetch the charges needed from that safety hole outside the adit. He stuck a yard of dynamite down each hole, not having call to stop and read the lettering on the greasy paper casing since they all knew what he was doing.

Trevor tamped some of the higher holes with clay for him. He bent over to pick up the lantern as he touched the tip of his lit cheroot to the master fuse and said, "Fire in the hole."

The stocky Drake waited until they were outside before he protested, "A foreman who knows what he's about usually clears the drift before he lights the fuse, you see!"

Longarm said he was anxious and sorry as they all moved clear of the adit. A few moments later the earth shuddered under them but most of the noise stayed in the ground. Longarm mentally kicked himself for having made too much noise with those earlier fake blasts. But mayhaps no harm had been done. Goldberg had been the only professional within earshot and he hadn't said anything.

Men moiling for riches tended to pay attention to their own beeswax. So that afternoon Longarm helped his hired crew muck, loading the "ore" in gunny sacks and loading them aboard the buckboard before he paid the boys off for their seven-hour shift and told them to consider the five hours he still had coming a bonus.

From the looks that passed between them, he knew he could count on them bitching at the bar as they drank their hard-earned dollars away.

They walked in with him but peeled off for the Crystal Palace as Longarm delivered his modest tonnage first to the assay office and from there to a reduction plant down the way when they told him he had medium-grade yielding mayhaps six or eight dollars a ton, or worth mining if you got help to work cheap and kept other expenses down.

He'd known that when he'd salted the face. He hadn't brought along enough gold leaf for a bonanza or many more loads of medium-grade ore. He had an excuse to seek working capital.

The old saw about a man needing a gold mine to work a gold mine had been based on the simple truth that finding the fucking gold was less than half your worries. You had to get the shit out of the ground and off to market without spending more than you could *get* for the fucking gold. Longarm knew of lodes, some rich lodes, all over the West where the gold still lay in the ground because there was no water to be found at any reasonable distance or the strike lay simply too far out in high impassible badlands to be worth astronomical hauling expenses. A mine got profitable as the coast of working it went down in proportion to the yield. A mine worked with the latest methods could show a profit on low-grade yielding less than a dollar a ton because it could deliver so many tons to wind up as a whole lot of slag and a steady trickle of gold ingots. It was what the paper pushers who kept the books called economy of scale. The rich got richer when each of their many hired hands produced a few cents more for a boss than they were paid, and that was how come the mine owners of Leadville were threatening to bring in the state guard and why Longarm as Canada Cooper was bitching about barely making enough to keep going with a proven claim.

After dropping that bait in the gloaming, Longarm went on to a late supper at the hotel restaurant to see if Molly had overheard how those two birds, Cooper and Skane, had stuck color.

She hadn't. But she congratulated him and said she'd known all along he'd been fixing to strike it rich. It was easy for him to strike a modest pose and allow it was too early to count all his chickens. It made him feel like a four-flusher to bullshit the mousy little thing.

He'd just cut into his pork chops when Buchanan T. caught up with him, grinning like a shit-eating dog. The Texican plopped down to say he'd just heard. "We were talking about how funny it would be if the two of us really struck gold, fucking around out on that abandoned claim! We're rich! We don't have to slave for Billy Vail out this way no more!"

Longarm glanced around, saw there were others dining with big ears all around and said, "Who's Billy Vail? Keep it down to a roar and we'll talk about finances later, in private, see?"

As if he hadn't heard, or didn't want to listen, Longarm's sidekick from hell went on. "Them two drillers we hired hit me for more money over to the saloon, just now. They said it hardly seemed fair you only paid a dollar a shift when the going rate is three and they drilled into profit for us. I gave 'em the four dollars they said they had coming. What's my share of the gold they mucked for us today?"

Aware others were listening and making the best he

could from a bad situation, Longarm said, "Too early to say. Weren't you listening when I explained how once the refined product winds up in the form of ingots stamped with their troy weights, the foundry credits us with the current market price, less their agreed on margin of profit?"

He forked down some mashed potatoes, drained his coffee mug and put enough silver on the table to pay the tab with a dime tip as he growled, "Let's get out of here. I ain't hungry as I thought."

Out on the street betwixt lamp posts, Longarm demanded, "Have you gone clean out of your head? You said we were working for Billy Vail in plain English!"

The towhead replied, "So what? I just said we weren't whoring for him nor anybody else now that we've lucked into a fucking gold mine!"

Longarm snorted, "Asshole, there ain't no gold in that try hole. That's why the ones who sunk it walked away from it, discouraged. I *salted* the fool hole in the ground. More than once. To make it look as if we could be drilling into ever richer ore, see?"

Old Buck couldn't. He said, "That's what Major Manson said, over to the saloon, when Trevor and Drake bitched about making us rich for piss-poor wages. The tinhorn said any man who bets cards he was never dealt might know other sneaky tricks. But old Drake told the major he was full of it. He said him and Trevor had drilled the face and helped you set the charges. Trevor allowed he'd tamped some of them and hadn't seen a pinch of salt shoved into form-fitting holes with plain old Hercules sixty percent. So what are you trying to pull? On *me*, I mean! I thought we'd both agreed any real gold we stumbled over up this way was our very own!"

Longarm started to explain. But on reflection he doubted it would be wise to confide in a man who'd just blurted Billy Vail's name back in that crowded restaurant. So he said, "Have it your way. I cannot tell a lie. I chopped down the cherry tree with my own little hatchet and we'll settle later, back in Denver when this is all over."

Skane grumbled. "The hell you say! Don't want to go back to Denver to do shit. Mean to go back to Texas in style, in my own coach and with rings on my fingers and bells on my toes!"

Longarm muttered, "Aw, shit," and strode on to the Crystal Palace with the beefy blond pest tagging along like a coyote worrying the flanks of a strayed buffalo calf.

They both got the glad hand all around when they came in together, as if they were pals. Knowing he wasn't welcome at the major's table, Longarm carried a scuttle of beer and a bowl of peanuts to another corner and sat down alone to see what might happen next whilst old Buck sulked at the bar, ordering stronger drinks.

What happened next unsettled him some. The handsome but dead-eyed Miss Rosemary closed down her faro layout and moseyed over to join him, her fandango skirts moving from side to side as they beelined towards him.

The henna-rinsed redhead in the low-cut velvet bustier knew she never had to ask permission to sit down across from any natural man. They called those French breastworks *bustiers* because they let a gal's bust show off to maximum advantage. Miss Rosemary produced a French cigarette in a long ivory holder and let Longarm light it for her before she blew violet-scented smoke in his face to declare, "I understand you bought that unworked Fordham claim out your way, too. Have you been peeking up the skirts of Mother Earth?"

Longarm truthfully replied, "Got it cheap. Figured it might be a good investment at that price. Ain't even tried to work it. Got a . . . friend just keeping an eye on the site whilst we work our deeper try hole. Can't say for certain either claim is worth the trouble."

She said, "I'll give you five thousand here and now for both claims in a bundle."

Longarm glanced over at her abandoned faro layout as he mildly asked if she might be a gold-mining gal.

The dead-eyed redhead answered easily, "I don't even care to wash dishes. Never panned for color in my life. I'm a sporting woman, as you may have noticed. I gamble for a living and gold futures are more exciting than any other game in town. So how about it? Five thousand, ready cash, as soon as you vacate both properties and hand over the transfer papers."

Longarm stared down at his suds as he demured, "I got to study on the offer, Miss Rosemary. I've heard the going price in these parts was low as twenty-five hundred a claim. But to tell the truth that strikes me as mighty low."

The dead-eyed gal sounded sure, as if she might know more than she was letting on, when she warned him, "You're not going to get a better offer. I'm offering you the going rate to save us both a lot of horse-trading and let me get back to my game."

She got to her feet, adding, "Think about it all you like. Mine the money out of the ground, a few dollars worth a day, or leave town with as much as our town marshal banks in four years!"

She turned to flounce back to her table, knowing full well how her hips moved under that fandango skirt. Buchanan T. came over, with a shot glass of bourbon in one hand and a beer in the other, to ask what all that had been about.

Longarm truthfully replied, "She just offered to buy us out. I figured somebody would. Never expected it to be her."

"What did she offer?" the beefy blond pest demanded.

Longarm said, "Same as they offered Goldberg. Five thousand for both. She's fronting for our mysterious Mr. Prince. Seems he don't allow anybody to bid on gold futures in these parts. I'm still working on how he keeps everyone in line."

The Texican marveled, "Five thousand and you didn't *take* it? My share comes to as much as that old Jew went home with. So let's sell out, split the five and let me go home in style, too!"

Longarm shook his head and said, "I'm trying to decide which fork in the road to take. It seems safer to sell at Mr. Prince's price whilst we try to find out who Mr. Prince might be. If we hold out he may show us what happened to others who held out. Means we got to get . . . Miss Nell off that other claim and out of town, whether she wants to wait for further news in Denver or not."

"Fuck your play pretty up in that covered wagon!" his nominal pard insisted, loud enough to turn heads as he swallowed the bourbon, chased it with a heroic swallow of suds and added, "I say take the money and to hell with everybody! I've never in my life had a shot at that much money in one bunch!"

Longarm snapped, "Shut your face! You're drunk and rolling all over the deck making foolish noises! I told you we'll talk about it later, in private, God damn your eyes!"

The out of control Skane sobbed, "God damn your own eyes! What sort of fool do you take me for? I know what you're planning to do. You're planning to take the money and run!"

Longarm got to his own feet and stepped around the table to warn his old pal, Buck. "You are way out of line. I don't mean to say that again. I want you to shut the fuck up, go back to camp and wait for me to tell you the whole story in private, after we both cool down and sober up."

Skane started to say something else.

Longarm said, "Now. If you blow what we came to do here I'll carry you back where we came from to face the music. That's all I have to say, right now. Go thou and shoot off thy mouth no more!"

He stood his ground until Skane sniffed it wasn't fair and wandered off through the blue haze of tobacco smoke.

Longarm saw others were watching him. The white-haired Major Manson was talking with Miss Rosemary over at her own table. Hoping to smooth his exchange with Skane over, Longarm picked up his own beer and took it over to join others bucking the tiger or getting taken by a henna-rinsed but beautiful gal with eyes cold as those of death incarnate.

So naturally Longarm's back was turned to most of the crowd in the smoke-filled saloon when Major Manson, of all people, suddenly gasped, "Hold on! Don't you dare!" And, since he hadn't shouted as much at Longarm, Longarm crabbed sideways as he spun around.

So the first shot from the Dance Brother's six-gun of Buchanan T. Skane missed its intended target by a whisker and scared the shit out of a gent playing faro when it plucked at his sleeve and shattered the window beyond.

Skane never got off a second shot. One round from Longarm's Schofield took him just over the heart and a second hit dead center to stagger him back and then back some more until he landed in the sawdust like a half-empty water bag with his twisted mind making way more sense as it stopped chasing fame and fortune forever.

Chapter 15

The already crowded saloon got more so as Buchanan T. Skane's life's blood and bladder contents were absorbed by the sawdust he reclined upon. Marshal Ellison elbowed through the crowd with a brace of deputies in his wake and his own gun drawn. Miss Rosemary called out, "It was a fair killing, Dave. The big blond buck on the floor started out to shoot his own pard in the back just now!"

The town law regarded Longarm with one eyebrow cocked as he said, "He must not have had much practice. What have you to say for yourself, Canada?"

Longarm had already reloaded and put the Schofield away. He wasn't sure where his scuttle of suds had wound up in the sawdust. He shrugged and said, "I'm still trying to figure out what just happened. I'd likely be the one on the floor if Major Manson, here, hadn't warned me in time!"

He nodded at the white-haired card shark to say, "That's one I owe you, Major!"

Manson grimaced and replied, "What can I tell you? I wasn't thinking. Threw a line to another kid drowning in a mill pond when I was little and I never liked *him*, neither!"

Another regular volunteered, "I might have seen more

of it, Marshal. The two of them had been arguing over the mine they've been working. I thought it was over, too. Canada, yonder, had turned away to come over this way when all of a sudden his pard was slapping leather on him from behind! Major Manson saw what was happening and yelled. Old Canada spun like a ballerina as the treacherous loser drew and fired first. I have seen the mountain and I have seen the hill, and I've never seen a faster draw nor straighter shooting from the hip!"

Another jovial voice opined, "Don't never throw down on old Canada if you are interested in a protracted existence!"

There came a resounding round of agreement from the crowd assembled. So Marshal Ellison told Longarm, "You ain't under arrest. But I hope you understand you ain't to leave town until our deputy coroner hands down his findings?"

Longarm said, "I ain't going nowheres. I got a gold mine here in Pot Luck."

The town law dryly said he'd heard. Then he turned to his own sidekicks to tell them he wanted the remains carted over to the town morgue for now.

He asked Longarm if anyone else was likely to come forward for the body, once the deputy coroner was through with it. Longarm allowed he'd get in touch with a mutual pal who knew some of old Buck's kin. He knew it would sound maudlin if he asked them to put a man he'd just gunned on ice, embalmed. He'd leave it for Henry to see the proper authorization arrived before old Buck got gamy.

The body still lay there and others were coming in for a gander as the dead-eyed Rosemary took Longarm by one elbow and murmured, "Walk this way."

He told her he couldn't walk that way had his life depended on it. She didn't laugh. She likely heard that often. She led him through the tobacco smoke and swirling humanity to a back room, where she shut the door after them and bolted it from the inside.

The back room was only furnished with chairs and another card table. She sat him down in one chair, cocked a long leg in a mesh stocking up on yet another chair with an elbow braced on her knee and told him gently but firmly, "My answer now stands at four thousand for both properties. I have a lawyer who can draw up the paper tonight and we can have you on your way before cockcrow."

Longarm smiled up at her and observed, "I admire a lady who thinks fast on her feet. But what makes you think I can't afford to remain a spell, Miss Rosemary? You heard the marshal tell me not to leave town and I just told him I wouldn't. What makes you think I might be wanted somewhere else?"

She said, "There's no might about it. Nobody gets that good with a gun without gaining a rep and nobody here in Pot Luck ever heard of a Canada Cooper. Ergo you have to be somebody else, visiting the town under an assumed name."

"I could be some famous lawman, traveling incognito," he pointed out, lest the thought occur to her as her own.

Rosemary answered without smiling, "Already considered that. A lot. Your dead pard bragged upstairs about toting a badge down Texas way. So how many lawmen shoot one another on mysterious secret mission?"

Longarm sighed and said, "He told the gals upstairs we were on some secret mysterious mission?"

The dead-eyed faro dealer said, "Everybody figured he was a blowhard. *He* sure figured wrong when he decided to blow *you* away. So fess up. Who are you, really? Anyone can see you're an old pro with that Schofield."

He smiled thinly and replied, "I never shot nobody with this old army revolver. Just picked it up along the way because I'd heard there might be wicked boys, and gals, up this way."

She smiled back down at him with no signs of life in her ice-cold eyes to decide, "Have it your way. I'll give you

130

five thousand for the two unencumbered claims and you can tell them you're Little Jack Horner at the inquest if that's your pleasure."

She let that sink in before she added, "If you *were* somebody with a rep, not wanted too badly in other parts, there could be a future for you here in Pot Luck."

Pretending not to follow her drift, Longarm asked, "You mean, after I sell my claims and they tell me it's all right to mayhaps try my luck up around Buckskin Joe where that lucky cuss, Old Harris, wound up with his bottom on a flying carpet of gold?"

"I told you I only invest in gold futures, buying out underfunded claims and reselling them at a profit to the bigger outfits," she said.

"Nobody recalls the first name of Old Harris. He was a market hunter, not a miner. He was hunting deer down by Buckskin Joe, named after a mountain man who dressed that way after it was out of style," Longarm said.

"Damn it, Canada . . ." she fumed.

Longarm relentlessly continued, "Old Harris pegged a shot at this deer and missed. Missed with a rifle ball that might have still had some killing left in it. Went scouting in the grass for his spent shot and found a long yeller streak in the green sod where his shot had plowed through grass roots to a stop."

She insisted she didn't care.

Longarm went on to say, "Old Harris parted the grass with his fingers to see it formed a shallow turf over a carpet of gold. Not blossom rock nor any other ore, mind you. A sheet deposit of solid gold alloyed with some iron, spread out just under the grass roots for acres and acres in every direction."

"Heavens!" Rosemary said, interested in spite of herself.

"Old Harris knew zilch about mining. He was a man who shot critters as a rule. But he knew what gold was when he saw it shining up at him. So he commenced to pry it up, like carpeting, filling pots and pans or anything handy, including his spare boots. He never filed a claim. That's how come his name's so uncertain.

As the prying up turned to digging harder, Old Harris sold any rights he had to a regular mining man and wandered off, rich. There was enough iron-gold left to support all the real miners and folk like you all, who moved in as Harris was leaving. Old Harris had made that one big lucky strike that inspires so many to grub like worms in the dirt for the color scattered like chicken feed when something awful happened to these mountains long ago."

"I know somebody who pays well for . . . peace and quiet," Miss Rosemary said when Longarm had finished his story.

Longarm laughed and asked, "Do I look like any peace officer to you?"

She laughed back, mirthlessly, and suggested they settle on whether he was ready to sell those two try holes or not.

He replied he was still studying on it.

"Don't take too long, Canada," she said, "You may wind up sorry you never struck when the iron was hot."

As Longarm rose to his feet, he slipped an arm casually around her waist to ask how hot other things might be.

She calmly replied, "Down, boy. You could never afford to hold my hand and, if you could afford to hold my hand, you'd be better off not holding it. This girl is spoke for and whilst I'm sure this will surprise you, there are more dangerous men than you by far in these here hills."

Longarm allowed he'd heard as much and backed off gracefully. He'd only made the move to see if he could find out what he'd just found out. He'd been wondering where a faro-dealing gal might have been inspired to invest in mining futures.

So Mr. Prince had told all his underlings to offer the same set price, with no competition allowed. That left who he was and how he ran such a tight ship from somewhere out of sight. But Longarm was getting a tad warmer.

Making his way on out through the crowd, Longarm left the mules and buckboard in town to walk home in the dark alone, hoping he'd be able to explain to Risa but afraid she'd have heard by now. You could hardly shoot anybody in a small town without it getting all over in no time.

Risa had heard. And she'd taken things the way he'd hoped she might not, he saw, as he read the note she'd left for him on a pillow in that covered wagon, once he'd lit the lantern to find her gone—bag and baggage.

When a gal who'd given a lover French lessons addressed him as "Dear Canada," he could tell how politely pissed off she'd been.

She said she was headed up to Leadville to see if she could hire a private detective who'd be serious. She seemed to feel men fighting to the death over her was silly.

Things could have panned out worse. He'd miss her bright eyes and sweet smile, but things were looking up, now that he only had his own back to worry about. That was the way he'd wanted things in the first place. He felt sure he'd have cracked the infernal case by now if Billy Vail had let him mosey on up the narrow-guage line and do things his own way.

He was wrong, of course. None of the earlier investigators sent in by state or federal agencies had gotten half as warm because they'd been *expected* to mosey in and poke about.

That was what lawmen did.

But as Longarm spread his bedroll on the gentle slope inside the adit of his try hole, he was the topic of discussion in an unlit office overlooking the address where Mr. Prince worked by daylight under another name.

Mr. Prince was seated in the dark behind an office desk with his own six-gun atop it in front of him, even though he

133

trusted Marshal Ellison and the dead-eyed Miss Rosemary as much as he ever trusted anybody.

Rosemary was filling them both in on her back-room conversation with Canada Cooper, leaving out the mild play he'd made for her because men could be so childish about such matters.

"I'm sure he'll sell at your price, Mr. Prince," she said. "He and his dumber sidekick barely made enough to break even after a good many wasted days drilling plain old rock. The one from Texas had gold fever so bad he feared Canada was out to cross him. Or mayhaps he was only out to hog all the color for himself. We'll never know, for sure, now. But that's the way some men get around girls or gold."

Marshal Ellison said, "Try her my way. Friends at the hotel restaurant heard Buck Skane mention U.S. Marshal William Vail by name and before that he told Greek Gloria he was a lawman."

"A *Texas* lawman," Rosemary pointed out. "And you said when you wired the Texas Rangers they had him down as a big kid playing cowboys and Indians."

"I hadn't finished," Ellison said. "What if they *started out* as lawmen hired by, say, the Bureau of Mines to pester us about those other claims we . . . bought out? What if they took over a claim to just look like a couple of mining men and then what if they really struck color and they fought about whether they should go on working for the law or just get rich?"

Rosemary sniffed and asked, "What if the dog hadn't stopped to shit as it was chasing the rabbit? When you think of all the what-ifs that go with the sporting life, you take in laundry and never take chances no more. Canada Cooper, whatever his name may be, is a sportsman. I'll stake my life on that."

Mr. Prince purred. "I know. I find it hard to buy an undercover lawman who shoots sidekicks as part of his dis-

134

guise. But he's not our problem, until he says no for certain. That *Swede* is our problem. He's *said* no for certain and he's sitting on silver chloride dusted with gold. I need that claim to consolidate what we've sewn up at that end of this field. Why don't I have it, Marshal?"

The town law said, "I told you. Lars Swensen has been up this way long enough to have done some adding up. He sent that letter to the infernal *Rocky Mountain News* advising them I was the one who'd know what happened to him if anything happened to him. I told the smart alecky reporters who asked that Lars Swensen was just a crazy old Swede with a marginal mine nobody wanted. I think they bought it. But how's it going to look if the Swede turns up missing with somebody else working his claim?"

Mr. Prince replied, "Nobody will be working his claim until I feel ready to consolidate all my apex holdings. You won't be the one Swensen transfers his claim to when he . . . leaves. If you plan things right you've no need to be in town when Lars Swensen . . . sells. You can be down in Denver in front of witnesses when Lars Swensen . . . leaves."

"It ain't that simple," Ellison said. "You don't send a boy to do a man's job and I'm not certain I'm ready to tell the children what goes on at night after we've tucked them into bed."

When Mr. Prince just sat there pensively, Ellison quickly added, "I never said it can't be done. I only said I wanted to study on it a spell."

"You do that," Mr. Prince said. "I want that Swede's claim in the hands of an . . . associate within forty-eight hours. I don't care how. This meeting is adjourned for now."

As they both rose, Mr. Prince said, "I want you to stay a while and suck my cock, Rosemary."

Marshal Ellison kept going. Nobody had asked for any comment. As he left, the dead-eyed beauty softly asked, "Did you have to put it that way in front of old Dave, Mr. Prince?"

The shadowy figure behind the deak asked innocently, "How else was he to know you suck my cock and not his? What are you waiting for, Miss Rosemary? Didn't you hear me tell you to suck my cock?"

She had. As she knew he expected, she came around the desk and got down on her knees as he swung around in his chair for her to unbutton his pants.

As she took what he had to offer in her mouth, Mr. Prince purred, "Faster. Deeper. And when I come I want you to swallow."

So Rosemary sucked him off as best she knew how and when he came in her mouth she swallowed. She knew better than to argue with Mr. Prince.

That was one of the things he liked best about being Mr. Prince.

Chapter 16

Longarm had just enough gold leaf left to salt a couple more blasts. He hired Trevor and Drake to drill deeper, feeling trapped betwixt a rock and a hard place.

He suspected Rosemary would withdraw her offer if she got word his color had bottomed out so suddenly. But once he sold out he'd have no sensible excuse for hanging around.

The prospects around Pot Luck seemed marginal and prices all over the hard-rock mining country were too insane to encourage tourism or retirement resorts. Jerry-built hotels with gaps in the siding and pack rats in the rafters charged four bits more a night than tolerable hotels with indoor plumbing down Denver way. You could order a full course meal for seventy-five cents down yonder and get charged a silver dollar for little more than a snack in Pot Luck.

At the same time, carpenters made three-fifty a shift, miners three, and common laborers were lucky to make a buck for a twelve-hour day. So there was an uncommon demand for more affordable second-hand goods, and Longarm was able to unload the wagon, bedding and duds left by Nell Fordham for a fair profit, with a clear conscience, when he considered he'd bought Nell out and never screwed her in any way, shape or form.

The fact that he seemed to be clearing out his holdings was noted and approved of in other parts. He considered ending with the famous bang of old Jim Dexter in Leadville, who'd bought the Robert E. Lee claim for fifteen thousand, worked it like a beaver for months without producing an ounce of shit and convinced himself he'd bought a mountain of pure rock.

When the disgusted Dexter accepted a mite more than he'd paid for the Robert E. Lee and walked away from it, he never bothered to shoot his last charge of dynamite. So the new owners blasted the next morn and mucked out a $125,000 in their first day on the job, with the labor costing them sixty. It took a score of workers to muck that much high grade.

Others, of course, had not been that lucky. The mining game seemed designed by a lunatic to be played like blind man's bluff. Properties and mere options to mayhaps buy properties could sell for millions as desperate prospectors sold for next to nothing. It was still debated whether Silver Dollar Tabor had grubstaked George Hook and Gus Rische to sixty-four dollars worth of grub or seventeen and a bottle of whiskey. But that was how Hod Tabor had wound up with his Little Pittsburgh, which he later sold for a cool million along with shares in a bigger outfit.

They said his ten-million-dollar Chrysolite Mining Company had cost him an additional investment of six hundred dollars.

Mines yielded thousands a day, dollars a day, pennies a day or tons of nothing worth mention. So it wasn't how much Mr. Prince was offering through his dummy investors, but what might have happened to the ones who'd said *no*.

The hell of it was, nobody could say for certain anything had happened to the ones who'd said no, if they'd said no. Folk wound up missing all sorts of ways in mining coutry. You needed mortal remains to say anyone had done anything for certain, and why would a prospector who said yes hang around looking for those who'd said no?

The answer was offered to him the night before he figured he had one last salted shoot to go.

Having delivered another day's modest production, there being barely enough color in the tonnage to pay for hauling it in, he was nursing a beer in the Crystal Palace after supper when one of Rosemary's shills, a dapper little gent who won at faro beyond the natural odds of chance, came over to join him, offering to buy a round as he asked in a desperately casual tone if "Canada" had thought over Miss Rosemary's offer.

When Longarm allowed he figured on finishing out the week before he gave a final answer, the shill chuckled and said, "Say no more. She's a pretty little thing, once you look at her twice."

Longarm had no idea what the shill was talking about. So he sipped some suds and replied, "Say no more is the way I was about to put it."

The shill nodded knowingly and said, "I ain't the only one who's seen the way you pretend not to know one another when she serves you your supper . . . after taking her home from that vigil at the church the other night, late at night, you sly dog."

As the penny dropped, Longarm laughed and then sheepishly admitted, "Hard to keep a secret in a town you can spit across with the wind at your back. But, like I said, it's early, yet."

"I admire a man who looks before he leaps," said the shill. "But mind you don't take too long, lest you wind up with nothing, like that jackass who starved to death betwixt two hay stacks, trying to make up his mind which might be best."

So Longarm nodded at the dead-eyed Rosemary the

next time she looked his way from her faro layout, and they were in the back room again with her reaching under her fandango skirts to produce a folded sheet of legal bond for him to sign.

He read it over, twice, to make certain he was only agreeing to an option, with the actual transfer to be signed at the bank and a certified check to be handed over and cashed then and there or safely down in Denver in the sweet by and by.

Longarm felt obliged to warn her it was understood he'd have time to load up his buckboard and move out, leaving her both claims as they were, for better or for worse.

"You can come out and watch me shoot one last time before you take possession, or you can take possession and take your chances," Longarm said. "All I'm promising is two holes in the ground and I never said I found a wooden nickel in the former Fordham claim, Miss Rosemary."

She dimpled with her eyes, never changing expression as she replied, "I don't even have to see those holes in the ground. Others have assured me they're there and I make no bones about my plans for both. I mean to hold onto them as this mining district develops and sell for more than I paid when prices are higher."

"What if they go lower, ma'am?" he asked.

"Mining futures seldom go lower," she replied. "They're not making any more color in these mountains. Men who held on, or bought more, during the depression of the early seventies dwell in marble halls these days. Will you be taking Molly Boone away with you, Canada?"

He truthfully replied, "We ain't that far along in our courting, if you want to call it courting, Miss Rosemary. I reckon I ain't been as poker-faced about Miss Molly as I thought I was. But to tell the truth I ain't sure she's fully aware of my . . . plans for the future."

He wasn't *sure*, but it almost looked as if he'd seen a flicker of life in the faro-dealing gal's dead eyes. Mayhaps no more than the outline of a curious shark coming closer through murky water.

All she said was, "Your chances might improve if ever you saw fit to spring for a store-bought shave and a haircut. Especially the shave. You look more like a wolverine than the froggy come-a-courting."

As he bent over the table to sign the option with the tricky fountain pen she'd materialized from nowhere, she added, "I suppose a poor drab stuck with waiting tables finds your beard distinguished. A woman can put up with most anything if . . . she has to."

He held the new-fangled invention up to the light to ask how it worked. She dismissively replied, "How should I know or care? I know you unscrew the nib and reload it with an eye dropper dipped in ink. A business associate loaned it to me, knowing I might get you to sign in ink tonight."

He gave her back the fancy writing instrument as she put the option in an envelope and turned her back on him to make it vanish. He knew she couldn't be keeping all that stuff where a dirty mind might expect. She likely had holsters and billfolds strapped to the insides of her thighs. Stuff like that would show under her skirts if she wore them on the outside of either gartered limb.

He agreed to meet with her, her lawyers and a notary the following noon. Then they went out to rejoin the crowd in the Crystal Palace. He turned down her invite to buck the tiger at her table. She almost laughed when he said he was willing to trust her in a mineral deal but not with a faro shoe.

He moseyed over to ask if he might get into Major Manson's poker game. The white-haired professional said, "Not hardly. Just because I saved your ass doesn't mean I'd trust you near me with a deck of cards."

As the others at his table laughed, Manson elaborated, "Guns are not the only things our Canada Cooper performs magic with. I'd tell you kids what I figured out after losing sleep. But I don't think any of you are old enough, and don't sidle around to read my hand, Canada!"

Longarm laughed and moved on. He spent some time bullshitting at the bar, trying to get somebody to start up about the mysterious Mr. Prince. He wasn't able to. The mastermind who seemed inclined to have his way with you or kill you didn't seem interested in the usual grafts and shakedowns of most mining camps. If he'd cut himself in on any vice and gambling, save for getting whores and gamblers to front for him, it didn't show as local gossip. And they usually knew in small town saloons and barber shops who the boss of the town might be.

Closer to closing time at that hotel restaurant, Longarm moseyed over to order coffee and donuts off little Molly. He sat there dunking donuts to where others were grinning and Molly was starting to look flustered.

She blushed red as a beet when he offered to escort her home from work. He waited under a lamppost by a side door, where he was meant to be seen. And when she came out with a knit shawl around her shoulders against the cool of a summer night at that altitude, he could see by lamplight she'd rouged her cheeks.

The fresh slathering of lilac water she'd treated herself to smelled pretty, too.

He knew others would notice, and remember, as he walked Molly home to her tar-paper shack, explaining along the way how he figured on selling his claim and asking her if anyone had been talking about that earlier on.

Molly said, "No. Nobody mentioned your name at all this evening. Does this means you'll be . . . moving on soon, Canada?"

"May stick around a spell," he said. "Got some loose ends to tie up and other prospects to study on, up this way."

She linked her arm in his as they passed two ladies of the evening on a corner and said, "Oh, I thought you'd be tagging along after Miss Theresa. She dropped by the hotel earlier to see if they had mail for her and when I served her a bite, she allowed she had time before she caught a narrow-guage."

Longarm asked if Risa had said whether she was bound for Leadville or Denver.

"She never said. Didn't she tell *you*?" Molly replied.

"Not hardly," Longarm said. "It ain't as if we had an understanding about such matters. I was only helping her look for her brother. I wasn't much help. So I reckon she'll ask somebody else."

"Oh, I guess I ought to be ashamed of myself," Molly said. "But I thought the two of you might have been sharing some of that mortal turpentine." She didn't sound as if it had upset her to hear she might be wrong.

And so things went, sooner than Longarm wanted them to, as time was inclined to pass when you were having fun. It was a caution how slow a minute could pass in a dentist's chair whilst it seemed to take no time at all to walk a pretty gal home.

Provided that was all you wanted to do with her.

Molly Boone was above-average pretty if you liked 'em sort of mousy and Longarm had long since learned it was the little shy-acting gals who were inclined to screw the liver and lights out of a man, if ever he got one started. He suspected librarians, schoolmarms and gals who waited tables and such stored up hankerings as they daydreamed some, waiting for some man to get them started.

But when he got her to her tar-paper cottage and she smiled up in the dark mysterious to invite him in for some . . . coffee, Longarm couldn't do it. He liked his cherries fairly green, but he didn't pick 'em and he knew she'd been waiting a spell for some prince to come along on a white horse and take her away from all this.

When he suddenly gasped and snapped his fingers, Molly naturally had to know why. "It just came to me that Mr. Prince can't be this real name. Mysterious masterminds

143

too shy to come out in the lamplight never use their right names. So he just *asks* his followers to call him that and I suspect I know where he came up with the fool name!"

Molly suggested he come inside and tell her all about it.

"Not tonight, Molly," Longarm said. "It's too early."

Molly replied in a puzzled tone, "You call this early? You sure talk funny, Canada. I want you to tell me more about Mr. Prince, durn it!"

Staying put outside her door in the dark, Longarm explained, "*The Prince* is a famous book writ by a weary old Italian diplomat they called Niccolo Machiavelli, a decent cuss disremembered as a devil because so many devils just read *The Prince* and take it as a book of instructions!"

"Oh, ain't it?" Molly asked, as if she knew what they were talking about.

"It ain't," Longarm said. "It's what they call an exposé. Mr. Machiavelli was making some points about politics when he laid out all the dirty tricks a real piece of work called Cesare Borgia had pulled to claw his way to top dog of a vicious pack. Rascals who've discovered *The Prince* in plain brown wrapping ever since never seem to read the same author's *Discourses*, which instructs folk how to *avoid* winding up under immoral dictators. Folk who call such rules *Machiavellian* forget, or don't know, old Niccolo favored a democratic republic as the only form of government that gives some of the people some of the time an even shake."

She yawned and asked what all that had to do with the Mr. Prince in Pot Luck.

"I suspect he read Mr. Machiavelli and missed the point," Longarm said. "He fancies himself an evil genius, ruling with an iron fist in a velvet glove. I suspect when I find out who he is, he'll turn out to be a bucket of slime pretending to be warm milk."

"Are you some sort of detective, Canada?" she asked. "You sure talk like some kind of detective."

He said he talked too much, kissed her without thinking, like a big brother, and was on his way as behind him Molly called out, "Come back here and serve me some mortal turpentine, you big tease!"

He hoped others heard as he headed on back to the worthless claims he was fixing to sell Mr. Prince through the faro-dealing Rosemary.

He was just as glad. The empty sites were starting to feel spooky in the dead of night.

But then, as he approached from the north instead of south, he saw a small night fire had been lit near the pitched tent, with his firewood, on his claim, by somebody acting like they owned it.

In sum, like somebody out to jump his claim.

So Longarm muttered, "We'll see about that," as he moved in slower, that army Schofield drawn and cocked in a serious fist.

Chapter 17

Longarm circled in as silent as an Indian to where he could see it was an Indian seated by the fire. The Indian looked to be the kid who'd been helping Goldberg drill, down to the south.

Knowing the customs of most nations, Longarm holstered his Schofield and let his heels crunch as he moved in without comment to have a seat across the fire from the kid.

After neither had spoken for a spell the Indian kid said, "Hear me. I am called Shunka Luta. You would say Red Dog. I am not Arapaho, Ute or Cheyenne. I am Absoroka. You say Crow. So it is not against your laws for me to work in Colorado."

Longarm nodded gravely and said, "If I was hiring, you'd have a job. But like your old boss, I've just been bought out."

When the kid didn't answer, Longarm went on, "How much does my little brother need to get back to his own people?"

Red Dog said, "I do not need any *mazaska*. The old *Wasichu*, Goldberg, gave me enough to keep me eating fat cow all summer before he went away. He had a good heart, for one of you. He told me he thought you and that other *Wasichu* you killed seemed *wastey*. The men who guard his old claim now do not know me. I ask you to tell them I am not *shika*. I do not want anything that is not mine. I only want to search for some *wakan* I might have dropped in the try hole. You call that medicine. Mine was strong medicine, handed down from my *tunkashila*, who was a shirt wearer. He gave me the claw of a *Mako Wakan*, a medicine bear, he killed as a boy with his own hands. I had it with me down under all that *maka* because I was afraid it might cave in on us. I think I must have left it there in all the excitement when we found there was yellow iron there after all. Today, when I remembered where I might have dropped my *wakan*, I went to see if I might find it. One of those new owners called me a thieving nigger while the other crept up behind me. He took me by the seat of my jeans and the back of this shirt and threw me on my face in the dust, outside the boundry markers. They both laughed. They said if I come around again they will kill me. But I think my *wakan* is down under the *maka* and I think I need a . . . *kola.*"

Longarm nodded soberly and allowed he was a friend to Red Dog, adding, "Might not strike them too friendly if we were to wake 'em up just now. I think you ought to spend the night here with me and come morning we'll go on over, I'll introduce you as a former employee, and explain about your grandfather's bear claw. I'm sure they'll agree it makes more sense to just let you look for your medicine than it does to cultivate needless enemies."

So he fed the kid some pork and beans and let him bed down in the tent as he crawfished down into the try hole, not expecting any trouble in the morning from sensible gents hired to keep an eye on things and likely confused by Red Dog's awkward way of expressing himself.

But by the dawn's early light, when Longarm moseyed over with the Indian kid cautiously bringing up the rear, that same bird with the double-barrel Greener waved the same at him to yell, "Back off, pilgrim! This here's the propery of Mr. Sam McSorley who owns the Diamond Livery as well and pays us not to entertain tourists."

As Longarm kept moving in, he circled so the rising sun was at his back and hence in the eyes of the surly shotgun-wielder. The same sun cast both their shadows to the west, where he could keep a casual eye on them. Moving in close enough for reasonable conversation, Longarm gently but firmly said, "Don't point that Greener at me. It ain't friendly. Yonder Indian kid used to work here. He thinks he might have left a pet bear claw in the diggings. It ain't worth nothing. But he sets store by it as a family heirloom. So what say we let him see if it's down there and, in any case, I'll not ask why the druggist sold a claim without working it."

Then, seeing he'd been keeping a better eye on shadows across the sunlit grit than had the thuggish asshole creeping up behind him, Longarm grabbed the double barrel of that shotgun so's he wasn't there when both barrels went off. He spun on one leg like a pissed off ballerina playing baseball with a discharged ten-guage.

The thunderous double detonation froze the one behind him like a statue. Using the shotgun, Longarm hit what might have scored as a sacrifice fly if the thug's head hadn't been attached and spun on around with the shotgun cocked for another mighty blow as he asked the empty-handed one still standing, "Want some of this?"

The one who'd pulled both triggers to no avail gasped, "Hell, no, let the kid have his fucking medicine if it means *that* much to you-all!"

Red Dog scampered into and soon out of the try hole with his grandfather's bear claw, and all was well with the world again as Longarm and Red Dog walked into town together. The two parted friendly near the place Molly worked. Neither had said anything. Neither had felt a call to. It was understood that only white men were served in certain establishments. Still, it was generally agreed Clay Allison had had no call to gun those three colored cavalrymen in one burst of gunfire as they came through the swinging doors of a hotel taproom down Cimarron way. Most knockabout gents would have just told them they couldn't drink there.

He dunked donuts and flirted with Molly so's it would show for a spell. Then he went over to the bank where, sure enough, the faro-dealing Rosemary and a lawyer who looked like weasel dressed for church waited in the back with a bank officer who doubled as a notary public.

As they were signing all sorts of papers in triplicate, the dead-eyed Rosemary asked him with a Mona Lisa smile how come he'd pistol-whupped those guards hired by her friend, Sam McSorley, to keep an eye on his new property.

Longarm modestly replied, "Never pistol-whupped nobody. Disarmed the one and flattened the other when they got smart with me. We got it all straightened out and parted friendly."

Her lawyer marveled, "This one took on Hansen and Duffy, alone, and nobody was killed?"

"Our Canada does that, too," Rosemary said. "Hansen and Duffy were lucky. Someday Canada is going to tell us who he really is. You might want to pass the word that, in the meantime, he's nobody to mess with."

The notary, who must have been halfway honest, objected. "Hold on, Miss Rosemary. I'm not certain a notarized document signed under a false name would stand up in court!"

Her lawyer responded, "You notarize the papers and let me present them in court, Tom. Anyone can sell any goods or service under any names they want as long as nobody charges any fraud. How do you think the late Rosanna Gilbert got paid for all that spider dancing and . . . other services as Lola Montez? Half the actors, writers and recent residents of our Golden West started out with other names in other parts. So if Mr. Copper, here, has a mining claim to sell, and nobody can prove it belongs to anyone else, he's free to sign it over as the Lost Dauphin of France."

As Longarm signed, the lawyer added with a chuckle, "Wouldn't it be something if he really turned out to be the Lost Dauphin of France. The fool kid must have wound up *someplace!*"

"Our Canada, here, is too young and if he *had* been the oldest boy of King Louis, their side would have *won!*" Rosemary said.

"Aw, mush," Longarm said.

Then she handed over the bank draft and the banker asked if he wanted to cash it or leave it with them to gather some interest.

Longarm put it away as he replied, "Neither. I reckon I'll hang on to it and cash it on down the road when I need to."

It wouldn't have been polite to say he was keeping the signed paper as possible evidence.

So he was free to go and went over to the same hotel to hire himself another room, seeing he wouldn't be staying out at the claims and he hadn't made up his mind whether he wanted to shack up with Molly or not.

He knew he wanted to jump her bones. She was pretty and he was a natural man. But after that she was mighty young, not too bright and likely to get false hopes up if a man who'd just sold a gold mine got to playing slap and tickle with her.

Leaving that bridge to be crossed when they came to it, Longarm next repaired to the Diamond Livery, where he found the burly Sam McSorley willing to shake and hear him out, but staring at him poker-faced as he explained about Indian notions of medicine and how he might have saved Hansen and Duffy more serious trouble by just roughing them up a mite.

He said, "The Crow are listed as friendly Indians, not sissy Indians. Before they split off from their Hokan-Siovan–speaking roots a spell back they were the Sparrow Hawk clan of the western Lakota. Some say they were more truculent and the sign lingo for what we call Sioux is a finger drawn across the throat from ear to ear."

"My boys tell me the punk was maybe sixteen, soaking wet," McSorley cut in.

Longarm said, "That's why he asked me to help him after your boys rawhided him. I know they had him down as a harmless punk. They acted stupid as hell around me. It's the harmless looking punks who are more inclined to kill than to arm wrestle. Red Dog had medicine on that property he wanted, and he was going to keep on wanting his fool medicine until he got it or somebody finished him off. But now it's over and nobody's dead and that ain't the main reason I'm here this afternoon."

McSorley didn't answer.

"The main reason I'm here is that I have a buckboard and two fair mules I have no use for, now that I don't have a claim to work," Longarm said. "I bought everything up in Jamestown, where prices are lower than they are down here. Might you be interested if I offered everything for no more than I paid up in Boulder County?"

McSorley said he'd have to see the buckboard and its team before he even thought hard about the deal. They shook on the mayhaps and parted friendly. Longarm went back to the hotel, undressed and took a flop with nobody watching. He'd read where some prime minister, asked to advise a recently crowned queen, had said, "Your Majesty, never pass up a chance to catch forty winks or go to the toilet. For one never knows when one may get another chance."

He awoke as the sun was setting, aroused by the changing light, and except for still needing a shave, bad, made himself presentable to go down and have supper.

Molly acted as if she'd missed him all day. He decided his best course, or at least the most decent course, would be to level some as he walked her home.

He took his time supping, downing plenty of strong black coffee he might need for later no matter how things turned out. Then he went out on Main Street to visit more parts of town whilst he passed the time. For he'd met an old sailor one time who'd been to most every port in the seven seas but couldn't tell you shit about the sights and sounds from Singapore to Hoboken.

In all the ports the sailor had visited he'd found one good barroom and one good whorehouse as close to the docks as possible and he'd always gone back to the same ones, every time he was in port. So, he could tell you how to get screwed, blowed or tattooed in Hong Kong or Honolulu but couldn't tell you why either port was there.

So Longarm ankled south as far as the narrow-guage stop, through the sprawl of reducing plants, smelters, coal yards, lumber yards, slaughterhouses or warehouses running 'round the clock to serve the still-sprouting mushroom known as Pot Luck.

Since those mines actually in production were worked twenty-four hours a day, seven days a week, your Sabbath be damned, someone was getting off or going to work at most any hour, and that was why the Crystal Palace and most of the other saloons were open all the time, albeit with changes of shifts since even whores slept now and again.

As he passed First Congregational close to ten, working his way north again, he saw candles burning inside indicating late services for some other dear departed. For such a new town, the fair-sized churchyard was commencing to crowd some. Longarm tallied twenty-seven headstones on the far side of the picket fence as he passed by. He figured there was room for thrice that many more, and then they were going to have to consider starting a municipal cemetery, like they had in Dodge.

Longarm had no way of knowing other eyes were interested in him as he worked his way along Main Street from one puddle of lamplight to another. As he moved on out of view, the man who liked to be called Mr. Prince turned from the window of the blacked-out office to sit down behind his desk. Just then, Marshal Ellison rapped on the door jamb to stand there, uncertainly.

Mr. Prince purred, "Events would seem to be overtaking us. Have you seen the classified ads in this afternoon's edition of the *Rocky Mountain News*?"

Ellison asked if they might be talking about Lars Swensens's offer to sell his Swedish Nightingale for a hundred thousand on the open market.

"We are," Mr. Prince said. "One of our associates is going to have to buy him out before some pest like Leadville Johnny Brown shows up to queer the do. I understand the stubborn Swede is alone on his claim, even as we speak?"

"Let all his help go," the town law said. "Forted up inside the adit behind sandbags, with a Gatling gun as if he's expecting company."

Mr. Prince chuckled dryly and replied, "As well he should. But don't you see that makes things simple? We'll have no witnesses to eliminate. After you and your boys tidy up, we'll have witnesses of our own who saw him off on the narrow-guage with his baggage and our generous offer. In times to come the check will be cashed back East and clear for us to present in the unlikely event we ever have to. Where are the snows of yesteryear? Who ever looks for Chicken George since he sold that salted claim to Hod Tabor and vanished in a haze of alcohol fumes? I want you to rid me of Lars Swensen. Now. I don't care how. Just do it. Let me worry about the paperwork to cover your tracks. Have I ever slipped up yet?"

Ellison sighed and replied, "Not yet. But not yet ain't the same as always and I fear Lars Swensen is on to us, Mr.

Prince! I fear he's figured out what you've been up to and what happened to them others!"

"All the more reason to get rid of him, fast!" he added in that stage whisper he affected. "I don't expect you to charge a crazy hermit as he aims a Gatling gun at you. You're the law. There must be dozens of ways for a lawman to get the drop on a man who's been calling for the law!"

Marshal Ellison shook his head to say, "It's too big a boo for this child, Mr. Prince."

So Mr. Prince shot him.

As gunsmoke drifted in the reverberating darkness, another follower came in to ask, "You rang, sir?"

The boss, who had the follower scared shitless, said, "Marshal Ellison dosen't work here anymore. Get someone to help you tidy up and dispose of the mess in the usual way."

He rose to his feet in the dark, adding, "I have to go out, now. When I get back I expect to see nothing indicating such trash was ever up here."

Chapter 18

The murderous shot had been heard across much of Pot Luck, but things were forever going bump in the night around mining camps and nobody paid much mind. So the one main street and myriad footpaths were at peace as Longarm walked Molly home a spell later.

Along the way he felt obliged to tell her at least as much as she had to know. He said he needed an excuse to linger in Pot Luck after selling his claim and repeated some of the gossip he'd heard about them.

She confessed she'd heard-tell she had a swain who needed to shave and allowed it didn't upset her all that much if he meant to grow him a beard.

He said, "The thing is, Miss Molly, I'll be moving on, alone, as soon as I'm done here. If the truth be told I'm still looking into the ways that Jacques Ferrier and mayhaps some others may have turned up missing."

"You mean you're still working on the sly for that Canadian lady I thought you might be sparking?" she asked.

He said that was close enough and added, "If you were willing to let me have them think we ... had an understanding, others might not wonder so hard what I was doing here, this late in the game."

"You mean if we was to pretend we was shacked up?" she demurely asked. He nodded and said, "It would give me all sorts of leeway to pussyfoot around. Of course, we'd know we were just putting on an act. But if you don't want to risk your reputation . . ."

She laughed bitterly and asked, "What reputation? Nobody in town ever looks at me. Nobody seems to know I'm there. What kind of an act did you have in mind? Don't you think I'm pretty enough for mortal turpentine?"

They were approaching her tar-paper cottage by then and when he said he found her mighty pretty but he felt concern for the way a pretty gal could get hurt, Molly swung him around to kiss him wetly and exclaim, "Bless my great horned spoon if that ain't just the nicest thing any man has said to me in a coon's age!"

Then she unlocked her door with one hand, hanging on to him with the other, and said, "You come right in this house and do me wrong, you big considerate brute. For I have been wanting you to do me wrong since first I laid eyes on you and we'll just see if you're man enough to hurt me!"

So, seeing she'd put it that way, Longarm went inside to take his beating like a man.

The dark interior smelled of soap and lilac water. The bed turned out to be a pallet on the floor, albeit piled with clean quilts and bed linen. She was all over him like a love-starved child of nature with neither shame nor reservations and he was in her before they could finish taking off all their duds. So Longarm just enjoyed what nature offered and never asked Molly where she'd learned to act so natural. Dissecting wildflowers under a microscope could take all the magic out of them.

Later, stripped all the way and sharing a smoke, Molly giggled and said he was teaching her wicked habits because she'd been dipping snuff a spell but wasn't used to *smoking* tobacco.

She never asked who'd taught him to smoke or do her

that way with her thighs together and her ankles crossed betwixt his, Lord love her. So he felt no call to ask where she'd learned to cross those same ankles behind the nape of her neck, with three pillows under her amazing ass.

Her ass was amazing, as was the rest of Molly, because she'd looked so mousy in her loose-fitting waitress uniform. It was too early to tell her some looked right *through* her, as she complained, because she was dressed like a frump and worked in a dump. He feared she'd take it wrong if he mentioned a wine theater run by a pal over in Leadville. To begin with he had to get *himself* out of Pot Luck alive.

Molly was better at bedroom athletics than pillow conversation but nobody can commit mortal turpentine, as she called it, hour after hour. So he found himself speculating on the mysterious Mr. Prince they'd both heard so much and knew so little about.

She's never heard of Niccolo Machiavelli, of course, but found the notion that somebody had written a whole book about another Mr. Prince so many years back right interesting. She asked how Mr. Machiavelli could have known Pot Luck's Mr. Prince would come along.

Longarm replied, "I doubt old Niccolo ever heard of the Rocky Mountains. But the dirty rotten cuss he described so long ago keeps coming along. I suspect a lot of 'em *read* that book by Mr. Machiavelli and misunderstand what the author had in mind. For as that Hindu *Kamasutra* is filled with all sorts of suggestions for sassy positions for . . . mortal turpentine, *The Prince* describes one dirty trick after another and advises, or warns, a ruler who means to rule folk ruthless that he has to make up his mind early on that there's no *nice* way to do it. The prince Mr. Machiavelli layed out for his readers warts and all didn't try to make folk *like* him. He figured they'd do just as he asked if they *feared* him. So he kept them that way by pulling cruel jokes, punishing folk unjustly and rewarding some by surprise whilst he spit on others. He wanted them jealous and spiteful towards one another, lest a new leader arise from among them. Whenever one of his followers *did* seem to be getting popular the prince got rid of him, dirty. He made sure it was understood that all things, good or bad, came down from and depended on him and him alone."

"He sounds like the head matron at the orphan asylum," Molly said. "Do you reckon she read that same book?"

"A lot of monsters must, seeing they all act much the same," Longarm said. "Henry the Eighth banned the book in England because he said there were too many good tricks in it. King Henry wanted to be the only one in England who knew them all. Both Napoleons are said to have admired Mr. Machiavelli's writings and neither appears to have read what he wrote about democracy. I suspect Mr. Bismarck, over in Prussia, read *The Prince* and understood it better. He sure made a sap out of Louis Napoleon in that Franco-Prussian war after he'd already messed up in Mexico, following sneaky instructions blind."

"What sort of a man was the original model? He sounds like a mighty poor tipper," she asked.

Longarm laughed and said, "You might be taken with him if he came into your restaurant for supper. Mr. Machiavelli describes him as a two-face possessed of convincing charm. Inclined to smile and look you in the eye as he slipped you poison from this ring he wore. His name was Cesare Borgia. The family was Spanish but they'd moved to Italy and none of them had any lifelong friends because everyone they made friends with tended to die young."

As if to show she read, Molly brightened and asked, "Don't Buffalo Bill have a famous rifle called Borgia? Lucy Borgia?"

Longarm laughed and said, "Lucretia Borgia, named for the kid sister of Cesare. Some say she might not have been as wicked. Some say she was just a beautiful, dumb blonde who did what she was told."

"What was she told?" asked the gal he was shacked up with.

Longarm said, "She mostly married up with noble gents of property. Then they'd die and their property would naturally wind up Borgia property."

He blew a fair-minded smoke ring and added, "Her last husband outlived her, likely because she died before her big brother could murder him. In any case, one can see why Buffalo Bill named a lethal weapon after her."

"What happened to her wicked brother?" she asked.

Longarm cheerfully replied, "Oh, he died before he could wind up ruling the world. He was younger than I am, now, when he got to feeling poorly and passed away. You tend to die young when nobody likes you. That's a point readers of *The Prince* tend to miss. Nobody likes you when you carry on like that."

She asked if he thought somebody was likely to poison their own Mr. Prince. He said, "Might be more fitting if somebody arrested him. He's in a position to answer lots of questions."

She asked if he meant to smoke and talk about Mr. Borgia all night. So he put the cheroot out and got back in her, even as he wished she'd let him drone on some. For idle pillow talk had a way of jogging a man's memory and he hadn't read Machiavelli for a spell.

As they got going again, he idly wondered where he'd been going with old Cesare Borgia until all of a sudden it hardly seemed important.

By the time they came again, he was too tuckered to talk. They fell asleep in one another's arms and she woke him early, so's he could do her wrong and let her get to serving breakfast at the hotel restaurant.

He had French toast and bacon there, whilst he was at it. When he led his mule team and trailing buckboard over to the Diamond Livery, he was pleasantly surprised. Sam McSorley offered him a flat hundred dollars and Longarm shook on it before the generous cuss could change his mind.

It got less mysterious when, handing over the five double eagles, the suddenly cozy McSorley suggested he go see his pal, the mayor, about a job opening that had just come up.

Mayor Gardner at the whitewashed city hall up the way looked like he preferred kissing babies to smoking cigars. He was smoking a Havana Claro and offered Longarm another as they met up in his office.

As Longarm lit up, the mayor explained their marshal had gone off to the Montana gold fields in pursuit of a better offer.

Mayor Gardner slyly suggested, "That's what some call kickbacks from houses of ill repute. Better offers. If you want his job it pays eight hundred a year plus the usual other considerations."

It was a tolerable offer. They both knew the other considerations were food and drink on any house in town along with extra bounties on papers served, arrests made and no questions about billing the taxpayers for the jailhouse grub provided gratis by beaneries who felt they ought to support their local law.

Longarm said he'd take the job. He didn't need the other considerations and doubted he'd be in town that many paydays. But it gave him a better excuse than Molly for hanging around Pot Luck and asking nosy questions. Questions didn't sound as nosy when the body asking them was the law. Folk expected lawmen to be nosy.

Within the hour he'd been introduced to his staff over at the nearby marshal's office and lockup. They had no prisoners in the back at the moment. He rated eight deputies. Four to work nights and four more to work days, with one always on hand at the desk and the others running errands or backing. "Marshal Cooper's" play. With nobody shooting up the town outside on an average day, Longarm allowed he'd let experienced help tend the routine chores whilst he moseyed about town, introducing himself and getting a feel for the job.

It seemed too good to be true. It likely was, he knew, as his first day on the job wound down with nobody ever mentioning Mr. Prince.

Longarm knew better than to bring up the subject of bogeymen under the beds in Pot Luck. He figured Mr. Prince would make himself known when it came to him.

He was right. Going on supper time he told his desk deputy he was on his way over to his hotel to freshen up and grab a bite.

Molly had served him, as a waitress, and he was working on corned beef and cabbage when one of the regulars from the Crystal Palace came in to tell him Miss Rosemary wanted a word with him, after sundown, around nine.

When he ambled over to the Crystal Palace a tad earlier, the dead-eyed redhead took him into that back room to say, "Congratulations. Good help is hard to find. But now that he seems to have found it, the man who runs things around here would like a word with you."

"Don't Mayor Gardner run things around here?" he asked, as if he didn't know.

Rosemary said, "Don't be silly. They call the man you're about to meet Mr. Prince. Before I take you to see him there are some things about him you ought to know."

"What country might he be a prince of?" Longarm asked with a smile.

She said, "Any country he decides on and he doesn't like dumb jokes. He doesn't like jokes at all and annoying Mr. Prince can be injurious to one's health. So when you meet him, just listen and let him do the talking. He'll tell you if he wants you to say anything. Let's go out the back way."

They did, following a cinder-paved maze of footpaths until she led him into the back door of an office building fronting on Main Street. When he asked what they did there in the daytime she said, "Business. None of it is any of your own. Mr. Prince keeps his various enterprises separate, with only himself knowing what everybody working for him might be doing. One more thing before we go upstairs. Mr. Prince pays top dollar for loyal service. I, for one, have never had as much money to spend in my life. But, *cross* Mr. Prince, and your life might not be worth spit on the walk."

He said he'd heard about such gents. He didn't say he had the bastard running Mexico in mind at the moment. She led him up to the top floor. A dark figure was seated in the hall with a shotgun across his lap. Rosemary didn't speak to him. She led Longarm into an office that seemed to be deserted for the night until the shadow behind the desk purred in a stage whisper, "Good evening, Marshal Cooper. It's so good of you to come. I feel certain you know your regular duties. I feel no need to tell you how to see to law and order in Pot Luck. However, I do have an extra chore for you. You'll be paid extra for carrying it out for me."

Rosemary had told him not to say anything before Mr. Prince told him to say something. So he just stood there.

Mr. Prince said, "I see you haven't started wearing the badge that goes with your position. You'll find one in your desk. I want you to put it on before you pay a visit to someone I've grown very tired of having in this mining district. His name is Lars Swensen. He thinks I'm out to buy his proven claim for twenty-five hundred dollars. He's wrong. I intend to pay you a thousand to get rid of him. Anyone in town can give you the directions to his Swedish Nightingale. The old crank has asked for help from the law. Wearing your badge and a friendly smile, you should have no trouble joining him in his fortified mine. When you do, I expect you to put him out of his misery. Are there any questions?"

162

Since he'd been asked, Longarm said, "Not hardly. Consider it done."

Mr. Prince laughed in a surprisingly boyish tone and told Rosemary, "You were right. He's just what the doctor ordered."

Then he asked Longarm, "Don't you want to know how we usually dispose of the . . . evidence?"

Longarm shrugged and said, "I work best alone. Two can keep a secret when one of them is dead. So let me worry about where I bury the bodies and I'll let you-all worry about the artistry with legal papers."

Mr. Prince chuckled and husked, "I like your style, ah . . . Cooper. I don't suppose you'd care to give us your real name?"

Longarm replied in an unworried tone, "Would you care to offer me yours, Mr. Prince?"

The whispering shadow purred, "Have it your way, as long as I get a Swedish nightingale *my* way. The bonus you have coming for the chore will be delivered to your hotel. I'll send for you if ever we need meet again. Rosemary will show you out. Don't ever wander around this building after dark on your own."

So that was that and as he left he still knew little more than he'd already figured out about their resident bogeyman.

Save that he was fixing to be in deep shit unless he produced a dead Swede or a reasonable facsimile, sudden.

As he walked Rosemary back to the saloon, he told her he figured on dropping in on Lars Swensen the following night. She agreed it sounded reasonable when he implied it was tough to sneak a body into a smelter before sundown. But as they parted friendly behind the Crystal Palace, the hard-eyed gal said, "Make sure you don't take any longer. Mr. Prince seems to like you. So you want to keep things that way."

Chapter 19

Having had to walk herself home and wait up for him a spell, Molly was in as close to a pout as her warm nature and natural good humor allowed. She forgave him and got on top. But once she'd come a couple of times, being a woman, she had to know where in blue blazes he'd been all that time.

Stretched out at ease with a cheroot betwixt his teeth and Molly's warm young body snuggled against his own, Longarm said, "Got to meet Mr. Prince in the shadowsome flesh. He's sort of spooky. He likely likes to play bogeyman. I doubt more than a very few of his followers have any notion who the two-face really is. He was behind my being offered the job of town marshal and in exchange he set me a chore the last marshal must have turned down."

He kissed the part of her hair and continued, "It's easy to see why. Our Mr. Prince is getting too sure of himself for his own good. Mr. Machiavelli warned about that. The ruthless cuss he chose as his example cut through the murky waters of Italian Renaissance politics like a shark through smaller fry but he burnt himself out in his early thirties. Such gents usually do. That's what you get from following books you admire to the letter. I mind the first times I stumbled across that Rubaiyat of Omar Khayyam, the Persian poet."

He chuckled and confessed, "I followed his instructions for a spell. It was fun. He said to eat, drink and forget about the future because tomorrow may never come."

She snuggled closer and said, "I like him better than Machiavelli."

Longarm said, "Old Omar can get you in trouble, too. For nine out of ten times tomorrow *does* come and there you are with a hangover, your best friend sore at you about his wife and all them bills to pay."

So the somewhat more prudent Longarm got Molly to work on time in the morning and put in an honest day's work as the law of Pot Luck. He knew they'd be watching him.

It was more tedious than challenging. Keeping law and order in a small town wasn't all that hard, most of the time. That was how come so many incompetents willing to work cheap lasted a spell as the town law until somebody like John Wesley Hardin blew into town.

That afternoon "Marshal Cooper" ran a deadbeat in on the charge of "theft of service" for trying to get out of town owing money. As he put the deadbeat away to wait on a hearing, Longarm advised him in a kindly tone, "Never try to skip town in broad-ass daylight, old son. You'd have done better catching that night train to Leadville. It comes through after midnight hauling mostly empty freight cars back from Denver. Hardly anybody expects to see anybody get on or off here in Pot Luck. But they notice, and send word, when a furtive stranger hangs around the flag stop in the sunshine."

Longarm supped at his hotel, warning Molly he had some night chores ahead, and considered checking the hell out and saving some damned money. But now that he had a better excuse for being in town he had no call to draw attention to his being shacked up with a local gal.

Well after sundown, having told his night crew he'd

check in with them around midnight, Longarm headed south along that granite reef in the gloaming with his new tin star agleam in the tricky light and the broad-brimmed gray cavalry that he now wore with cleaner pants set square.

As he approached the adit of the Swedish Nightingale, he saw old Lars Swensen had added a skull and crossbones to the posted warning over the adit. The immigrant had spelled *trespassing* as "TRACE PISSING."

When he was within ominous range of that Gatling gun peeking over a rampart of sandbags filled with tailings, Longarm called out, "Hello the claim! Marshal Cooper, here. I'm the law. I'm coming in friendly."

Getting neither an answer nor a burst of .45-70, Longarm sauntered on in as the tail assigned by Mr. Prince braced for the softer song of six-guns.

But no gunplay followed. Nothing at all seemed to be going on inside the Swedish Nightingale as the moonless night got ever darker. Then, as the church bell of First Congregational was tolling eleven, their new marshal slipped out of the dark adit to cut up to the footpath above and make his way north to Molly's place.

They were following him all the way.

At midnight, Mr. Prince was pleased to hear a search of the Swedish Nightingale had found it eerily devoid of Swedes. But a worked-out and flooded vertical shaft looked to have suffered a rock fall. If there was anything but ground water and rubble down that shaft it was hard to tell.

By that time Longarm and Molly were sharing a last smoke before they tried for some shut-eye. Longarm hadn't told Molly where he'd been so late, but this time, Lord love her, she'd forgiven him in the French manner.

Next morning, after he got her to work and she'd served him another swell breakfast, Longarm checked with the desk next door and found he had a note from Miss Rosemary, asking to meet up with her at the Crystal Palace.

When they met there in the back room, Miss Rosemary said Mr. Prince was mighty cross with him. She said he had neater methods to dispose of bodies and asked why on earth he'd thrown Lars Swensen down that mine shaft.

Longarm lit a cheroot to blow some smoke as he calmly replied, "Who says anybody threw Lars Swensen down any mine shaft. He could have fallen in by accident. It happens. But since you mention it, and there don't seem to be nothing of value in that soggy hole, the new owners might want to fill it in."

She said, "Idiot! Who said anything about the new owners being the *final* owners? That mine is about to change hands on paper, a lot, until it's tough to make out who the Swede sold out to in the first place. What if, some time in the future, somebody decides to see what Swensen was drilling into when he abandoned that shaft?"

Longarm shrugged, blew smoke and said, "I understand, when they were breaking up this rusty old steamship for scrap, they found the bones of a riveter and his helper, sealed in by accident betwixt the plates of the double bottom during construction. Nobody never figured how the poor souls had been sealed in alive to suffocate, pounding on the plates, as riveting went on all around."

He blew more smoke and added, "Nobody ever spent much time trying to find out. Bad accidents happen, building ships or drilling mines, and the shipbuilders I just mentioned had identification papers on 'em when they were questioned."

She said, "I'll tell Mr. Prince what you just said. But . . ."

"No buts!" Longarm cut in with a bitter tone. It was easy to feel pissed off at Mr. Prince. He said, "You were there when I was offered a thousand dollars to rid Mr. Prince of Lars Swensen. Do you see Lars Swensen around town this morning?"

She soothed, "He just prefers smoother efforts, is all."

Longarm sneered, "That's why he asks others to walk

around with Gatling guns for him. He's too smooth by half. It's way smoother to hire somebody else and go back on your word than it is to kill folk yourself!"

"He kills folk himself," she said. "Keep that in mind before you make any crazy accusations! Mr. Prince has never broken his word to any of us yet."

"I'm sure Marshal Ellison agrees," Longarm snorted, adding, "I see what he's trying to pull on this child. I fear he's going to get away with it, too. How do you sue a man you don't know for refusing to pay you for services rendered, in a mine, with no witnesses?"

He unpinned the town badge from his shirt and tossed it on the table with a bitter smile, adding, "Here. Give this back to him and tell him where he can shove it. I don't work free, even when the boss acts like a bogeyman and promises the moon."

The dead-eyed faro dealer said, "For heaven's sake, put that badge back on before somebody sees you without it! Calm down. Cool off at the bar on the house and check your mail this afternoon. I'm sure things will work out to everyone's satisfaction once I assure him you left no ID on an already mangled and soggy Swede!"

So Longarm grudgingly picked up the badge and she pinned it on for him, flirty, like a schoolgirl pinning her steady.

He knew she expected him to kiss her. He didn't. To begin with, he was supposed to be going steady with the sweetly dim Molly Boone. For another, there was something about this one's dead eyes that reminded him of the morning mists drifting across the fields of Shiloh in the eerie silence after the battle.

So instead of kissing her, after she'd pinned the badge back on, he stared soberly down at her to say, "Bad things happen to us. Don't they?"

She shrugged her bare shoulders and replied with a game smile, "You had to have been there."

They both went out into the taproom, where she opened her faro layout early and he repaired to the bar to order a plain draft with no whiskey lacing it.

Being it was a mining camp, others came in or out at all hours and nobody seemed to pay much mind to their new marshal leaving. He drifted in and out of other saloons, upholding law and order as he listened for interesting gossip.

He didn't hear much. At noon he went back to the hotel and told Molly he could go for a light snack of hash under fried eggs with extra black coffee.

As she served him, Molly archly asked if he figured on staying awake that night. He allowed the thought had occurred to him. She bustled off to the kitchen, singing.

When he checked at the desk, he found an envelope waiting for him in his box. It bore the logo of Vulcan's Forge Refining & Smelting Company. When he opened it he found a check from the same outfit, made out to a sum of one thousand dollars and no change to Canada Cooper for services rendered at either the refinery or smelter. The point was that Mr. Prince hadn't signed by any name.

Longarm put the check away with earlier evidence he'd gathered and went to see about a haircut. By then it was well past noon and the big barber shop he picked on Main Street was crowded as he'd hoped to find it. He went in and picked up a pink copy of *The Illustrated Police Gazette*, then took a seat handy to a spitoon to wait his turn.

He didn't need a haircut and didn't want a shave yet. But as he'd hoped, customers from all walks of life ahead of him had a lot to say about someone not present. Next to women over backyard fences, nobody gossiped like men in barber shops. Men tended to joke more in saloons, aware their tongues felt thick, and so they worried more about them slipping.

As the town law, Longarm made mental notes about a handsome dog who was looking to meet his maker early, messing with more than one mining man's woman during the midnight shift. But he was working his way close to being called next when a gruff cuss in a business suit, Lord love him, asked if anyone there had heard how much Lars Swensen might have gotten for his Swedish Nightingale.

Another there said he hadn't heard the Swede had sold, adding, "I read in the *Rocky Mountain News* he was holding out for big money."

The mining man who knew it all said, "He got big money. Understand Dick Eppingham, the dairy man, come up with Swensen's hundred!"

There came along protracted whistle. Somebody observed, "Must be more money in a dairy herd than you'd have thought!"

The barber said it was Longarm's turn. He rose to his considerable height, then he nodded and had a seat, allowing he'd settle for a trim and a hot towel shave.

He figured he owed it to good old Molly, seeing it was about over in Pot Luck.

As the barber leaned him back and got to work, Longarm reflected how, whilst the sales of Goldberg's claim and those two others hadn't trapped anybody into bending federal mining laws, the cat's paw, Eppingham, had just been party to a provable criminal conspiracy, and Longarm had the payoff from those underlings of the smelting outfit on paper and likely more than one body that could still be identified as well.

So it was midafternoon when a way-neater–looking Longarm made it to First Congregational and strode across its hospitable churchyard to the manse next door to the church.

The sexton who came to the door allowed the Reverend Ashton was in his back office, composing a Sunday sermon. When Longarm allowed he wasn't there to pray, the sexton led him through the living quarters, calling out in advance.

The Lincolnesque sky pilot who liked to be called Ash

came to the door to invite the new marshal into his own inner sanctum. It reminded Longarm of Billy Vail's, save for the paneling being knotty pine.

Ashton waved his visitor to a nice guest chair and perched on one corner of his desk to ask what had brought him to First Congregational that afternoon, adding, "I hardly recognized you without the stubble."

Longarm said, "I figured it was about time to end the masquerade. I am Deputy U.S. Marshal Custis Long of the Denver District Court on a special assignment for the Bureau of Mines. I am here to arrest you. I reckon you know the charges, Mr. Prince."

"I'm afraid I don't!" tried the sky pilot in bewildered innocence.

Longarm said, "It ain't going to work. Disguising your voice up in yon office across the way might fool some of the people all of the time but I suspect I've read more books by Niccolo Machiavelli than you have. You must have stopped at that one exposé so many of you sons of bitches seem to take for a training manual. But as we both know, *The Prince* was his thinly disguised description of Cardinal Cesare Borgia."

"I don't know what you're talking about!" insisted Ashton.

Longarm relentlessly went on, "It came to me the other night as I was describing Machiavelli's prince to . . . a pal. Old Cesare Borgia wasn't no regular prince. He was a *prince of the church*, in command of a Papal army out conquering other feudal holdings, the way most everybody with an army to call his own was inclined to, in them days."

"Do I look like a Roman Catholic cardinal to you?" sneered the tall Calvinist minister, if he was a minister.

Longarm said, "A modern Catholic priest would never get away with just setting up his own church out in the middle of nowhere's much. But it's my understanding the sky

171

pilots of your sect don't answer to anybody but the congregation that hires you. Or a wolf pack you can *call* a congregation who hired you. But we'll work out such details farther along. I have all I need to arrest you. Once we have you behind bars where you can't make faces at your congregation of cat's paws . . ."

"What congregation of cat's paws?" the sky pilot cut in, adding with a sneer, "Do you really propose to arrest over a hundred God-fearing men and women as some sort of evil cult?"

Longarm shook his head and replied, "Just your inner circle. We both know most folk here in town have been taking you for a real congregational minister. But out this way, it's all too easy to set yourself up as a doctor, a lawyer or a preacher with a private graveyard in his front yard."

"And I suppose you think you can prove one word of this pipe dream?" asked Ashton, smiling.

It was not a nice smile.

Longarm said, "Sure I can. I've got the bribe you paid me for the murder of Lars Swensen. That dairy man is fixing to shit when we ask him to account for Swensen selling him the Swedish Nightingale *after* your other underlings had already reported Swensen dead."

"How do you propose to get out of murdering Swensen?" asked Mr. Prince in sudden interest.

Longarm said, "I never murdered him. He's alive and well in Leadville and fixing to testify against you-all in court. I went over the night *before* your boys watched me bluff my way in past that Gatling gun and come out alone. Once I told Swensen who I was and what my plan was, it was no big deal getting him aboard that late train to Leadville a night *before* your boys watched me slip into his claim to kill him."

The two-faced sky pilot chuckled and purred, "Rosemary was right about you. You really *are* good!"

Then he added, "You'd better come out, now, Rosemary."

So Rosemary did. It wasn't too clear where she'd been hiding or just how she packed all that hardware under those flamenco skirts. But there she stood, with a Harrington & Richardson whore pistol in each hand and both of them trained on Longarm.

It got worse. That sexton came in with a bigger Colt Dragon Conversion and he wasn't aiming it at Rosemary or the sky pilot.

Chapter 20

Longarm smiled sheepishly and asked, "Don't this ever feel downright Machiavellian? This is where I'm supposed to feel scared and plead for mercy, right?"

The now-unmasked Mr. Prince rose to his own imposing height by the desk to purr, "As our mutual mentor, Niccolo, advised, a man of destiny doesn't give a fig for what others may *feel*, as long as they fear and obey him."

He let that sink in and added, "You will now tell me what else you think you have on me and mine, Deputy Long."

Longarm said, "Hell, ain't it obvious? Once I guessed who it had to be, the rest all fell in place and, like I told you, I've that paper trail leading back to you and . . ."

"I never signed one check you can connect with a mine transaction!" the mastermind cut in, hopefully.

Longarm shrugged and said, "Not direct, you sly dog. But once the bank examiners get to digging into the accounts of livery stable owners, dairy men and . . . faro dealers, no offense, Miss Rosemary, won't they find the grubstakes from your more substantial church funds? And won't most of your cat's paws turn state's evidence when presented with such incriminating records?"

He let that hang fire a spell before he added, "Why would, say, Miss Rosemary, here, want to stand trial for murder when all she'd have to say was that you put her up to buying some mining property for you in her own name?"

"None of my . . . followers will ever betray me!" thundered the sham sky pilot in the same tone John Brown might have used back in Bleeding Kansas to address his fanatic cult.

Longarm shrugged and said, "It's over, Cesare. It was over as soon as I saw you were one of those twisted bookworms who read *The Prince* and fail to heed its message. All of you get wrapped up in the dirty doings and miss the caution signs, like a goofy newlywed consulting the *Kamasutra* for thrilling positions whilst inflicting dreadful injuries on his bride."

"What did Lars Swensen tell you? I have ways of making men talk!" the creepy sky pilot cut in.

Longarm cheerfully replied, "Cardinal Borgia was good at making men talk. He had swell torture chambers set up and his victims told him just what he wanted to hear, whether it was true or not. So he was slicker, in my opinion, when he sent his trusted followers into a locale they'd just taken to torture half the town fathers to death!"

He chuckled and added, "It got them out of his way, whether they knew anything or not."

Ashton roared, "Fuck Cesare Borgia! Fuck his followers! Tell me about that fucking Swede!"

Longarm continued, "After the town had surrendered and all its big shots had been put to death, old Cesare rode in, wearing armor over his red cardinal outfit, to hold court and dispense justice."

"I hardly need a lecture on my own chosen namesake!" Ashton snapped.

It would have been dumb to point out he'd just admitted being Mr. Prince in front of potential witnesses, so Longarm turned to Rosemary to say, "Here's the best part. Af-

175

ter the man who'd ordered their town taken had its citizens fawning at his feet, he asked them if anyone had any complaints. It must have taken some prodding. But once a few had allowed they might feel put out by the death of a favorite priest, parent or whatever, old Cesare rose up on his hind legs to declare before God he'd never ordered anybody killed and then, to prove what a gent he was, he directed the first bunch who'd carried out his orders to be executed in public to the delight of all assembled."

Longarm chuckled and continued, "After he'd hung, drawn and quartered senior officers who might have been getting too big for their britches, old Cesare was in the catbird's seat with all his political enemies and possible rivals eliminated, grinning like a Cheshire cat."

He let that sink in and added, "The few followers left who weren't singing his praises as a prince of a fellow were too scared of him to say boo."

Then he smiled at Ashton, not unkindly, to observe, "He was going on thirty-three when it occured to the few followers he hadn't killed that he was out of control. His kid sister took to avoiding him, holed up in her own castle. It ain't too clear exactly who murdered him, in the end, but I reckon they figured somebody had to, don't you?"

Ashton said, "Rosemary, I'm going to ask him one more time what Lars Swensen told him. If he gives me a smart answer I want you to shoot him in his left kidney to gain his undivided attention."

Then he took a deep breath, let half of it out so his voice would remain calm and quietly asked, "Where is Lars Swensen at the moment and what did he tell you about our . . . offer?"

Longarm said, "Don't get your bowels in an uproar. It ain't no secret. Like I told you, right after you ordered me to murder the poor old cuss I went directly to his Swedish Nightingale and, finding him way easier to talk to, I snuck him aboard that late night train to Leadville."

"And so now he'd be . . . where . . . in Leadville?" purred Mr. Prince.

Longarm said, "Where nobody you might send could get at him, of course. I placed him under the protective custody of Town Marshal Matt Duggan, a lawman who never heard of Niccolo Machiavelli but has a whole heap of notches on his gun grips. Matt's one of them old-fashioned gun slicks who keeps score. I advised him you might send somebody after Swensen and old Matt just grinned, sort of hungry."

He paused before asking, innocently, "Are you fixing to send somebody after him, Ash?"

The self-appointed sky pilot didn't answer.

Longarm said, "I thought not. If you'd had any cold-blooded killers to send after Swensen you'd have never hired me the other night. You had the missing Marshal El-lison take care of those earlier victims. But you fired or killed Ellison when he lacked the grit to go on killing for you and so where does that leave you?"

Answering his own question, Longarm said, "That leaves you with all the paper trails leading back to you and a graveyard full of victims out front for you to account for, right?"

The man who'd wanted to be remembered as a mining baron if not as Mr. Prince heaved a vast sigh and decided, "You're right. I overreached. Next time I'll know enough to quit while I'm ahead."

Longarm shook his head to say, "Won't be no next time. You don't get up from this table to leave your suckers to pay the piper. You get to stand trial as the one murderous mastermind. But ain't that what you set out to be?"

Ashton shrugged and answered, simply, "Not any more. I'll be on my way, now, and you won't try to stop me if you know what's good for you. You'll have a seat and stay seated for exactly one hour. Then Rosemary and Frank, here, will turn you loose and we'll start all over, agreed?"

Longarm said, "Not hardly. I said you were under arrest and I meant what I said. Do you aim to come quietly or feet first?"

Ashton snarled, "That's it! You may fire when ready, Rosemary!"

So Rosemary fired, then fired again, and again, because she knew a .32 whore pistol fired with limited stopping power and her target was a very large man.

But he went down, as all men must, with that many rounds of any size in his chest.

As Ashton writhed on the floor at their feet, the sexton moved closer to finish him off with a heavier dose of lead before he declared, with all their ears ringing, "I follow your drift, Miss Rosemary. What happens now?"

Rosemary aiming the loaded revolver in her left hand at Longarm, quietly asked, "What happens now? Did I mention I happen to be ambidextrous?"

Longarm said, "What happens now is I write the two of you up for assisting me in the apprehension of a mass murderer. But take my advice and don't put in for any bounty money. I did hear you say, did I not, you meant to help your Uncle Sam clear up all the loose ends this dead cuss on the floor is in no position to help us out with?"

Rosemary said, "Neither Frank, here, nor I, nor any of the others had any hand in anything more serious than, say, forgery or fellatio."

Longarm nodded soberly and replied, "Never said you did. Do you reckon I can get the mayor, the coroner and such to go along with assisting me in tidying up this mess?"

Rosemary blinked her dead eyes and replied, "For the same deal? You can bet the farm on that!"

Then she stared up at him with just a flicker of life in her dead eyes as she decided, "You'd cut cards with the devil for a crack at your own notions of rough justice, wouldn't you?"

Longarm shrugged and said, "Rough justice is better than none and you can see it's the only game in town. It would take forever to cross every *T* and dot every *I* with both Ashton and Ellison dead. Meanwhile the heirs entitled to purloined property deserve the same, along with some answers about missing friends and relations. So why don't we send for the meat wagon, put this bogeyman on ice and commence cleaning up after him?"

So they did, and around a week later Longarm was seated in Billy Vail's office, down in Denver, flicking tobacco ash to the carpet mites as Vail went over his typed-up report some more.

Vail finally set the official report aside to fix his senior deputy with a keen look and decided, "You left some of the best parts out. Am I really supposed to tell the State of Texas that Buchanan T. Skane managed to get killed, innocent, in the cross fire of an attempt on your life?"

Longarm said, "Well, hell, *somebody* was out to shoot me in the back that time. Old Buck had been drinking and in all the confusion, who's to say just what happened?"

Vail said, "You. You were there and before you stick your foot in it there were others there who tell it different."

Longarm said, "Let's just remember him as he was, a sidekick from hell who started out on the right foot and got mixed up. I'd have *told* him what I was doing if he hadn't been such a total asshole!"

Vail said, "Thanks. I deserved that. But when I saddled you with him I meant it as a disguise, not a total disaster!"

Longarm soothed, "You had a point and in the end it worked. For as we put it together, later, I never would have gotten in with Mr. Prince if he hadn't had me down as a killer traveling under an assumed name."

He took a drag on his cheroot, flicked more ash and went on to say, "He was in the market for a killer. The only one he had, old Ellison, was a cowardly sneak who'd started to lose the little nerve he'd ever had. Once they

179

opened the door a crack to me, it got duck-soup simple. How many princes of the church with a handy graveyard could there have been up yonder? His pathetic playacting as a more famous villain he and so many others of his kind have always admired made it easier. His bogeyman act made it easier because of that process of eliminating you keep lecturing us about. Had he just acted like a mining camp thug I'd have had to cast a wider net. But I could see right off he was well educated and who but a well-educated and well-read man would pick such a handle as Mr. Prince for his fool self and then act the part like a fool? My first thought was some mining engineer with a smelter for the disposal of bodies. Then I noticed how tough it can be to run a smelter all by yourself with no witnesses. So when I met up with a possibly fake minister with a real grave-yard . . ."

"You say you recovered twenty-seven murder victims, all told?" Vail cut in.

Longarm grimaced and said, "It wasn't much fun. The legitimate funerals had involved fairly recent embalming. The bodies planted after dark with markers indicating they'd been wayfaring strangers taken in by a kindly sky pilot had not. But, like I said, none of the graves were all that old and it's surprising how recognizable most were, thanks to the cool boulder clay they were buried in."

He took another drag before explaining, "The coroner up yonder, once I assured him faking a county death cer-tificate was not a federal offense, explained how they'd made a mistake by burying murder victims in cold clay with no coffins. He said unembalmed bodies rot away faster in an air-filled coffin. Then he swore on his mother's grave he'd had nothing to do with any actual burials and I chose to believe him with a grain of salt."

Vail nodded and said, "I'm glad you found the remains of that missing newspaper man, and the remains of Jacques Ferrier are on their way home, now that you've recovered his profitable purloined claim. Is that what you were doing all that time up in Leadville, you sly dog, helping that pretty Risa Ferrier get a good price on her brother's lucky strike?"

Longarm honestly replied, "I never met up with Miss Risa in Leadville. She'd hired her own honest broker to dicker her a fair price and, last I heard, she got one. I had to help old Lars Swensen recover his own claim and after that, seeing I was headed up that way in any case, I had to help another pal out. She'd done right by me in Pot Luck and it would have been cruel to leave her there, after ruining her reputation in a small town."

He knew what Billy Vail was thinking. "I was trying to look like a hard-case drifter with no morals. Shacking up with a local gal might not have done it, alone. But combined with other shit-house luck I had with a whole bunch of assholes out to give me a hard time, it all worked out for me."

He flicked more ash and explained, "Betwixt tinhorns and toughs I had to back down and poor Buck going off his chump like that, I hardly needed mortal turpentine to convince everyone of my evil intentions. But like I said, this old gal did lay her rep on the line for me and I thought I ought to make it up to her."

"How, with more sweet romance?" asked Billy Vail.

Longarm innocently replied, "Oh, we'd had plenty of that down in Pot Luck. It took me some time to wrap things up there, and she said she'd been pleasantly surprised by the results of my first shave in weeks. So when we got up to Leadville I took her to the same beauty shop where Baby Doe and Belle Siddons get their hair fixed and their faces painted and it sure beat all how one visit to a beauty shop could turn a wallflower to a rambling rose!"

He chuckled fondly and went on, "After that we rambled on to a State Street couturier. That's what you call a place that sells fancy fashions from Paris, France, a couturier.

He took a wistful drag on his cheroot and sighed, "I

hadn't known what I'd be missing until I took her to this fancy wine theater and they hired her on the spot to greet and seat the Leadville elite. I'm afraid, to tell the truth, she was just as glad to see me go. She no doubt felt more free to strut her stuff, after our last night of mortal turpentine."

Vail answered, "Mortal turpentine? That's the second time you've made mention of the same. So what are you talking about?"

Longarm smiled softly to reply, "Have it your way: moral turpitude. But it was a heap more fun her way."

Watch for

**LONGARM AND THE
TEXAS TREASURE HUNT**

the 320th novel in the exciting
LONGARM series from Jove

Coming in July!

**Explore the exciting Old West with one
of the men who made it wild!**

**AVAILABLE WHEREVER BOOKS ARE SOLD OR AT
WWW.PENGUIN.COM**

GIANT-SIZED ADVENTURE FROM
AVENGING ANGEL LONGARM.

LONGARM AND THE
DEADLY DEAD MAN
0-515-13547-X

LONGARM AND THE
BARTERED BRIDES
0-515-13834-7

J. R. ROBERTS

THE GUNSMITH